Roseville's Blooming Lilly

With a smile!

Millie Curtis

Millie Curtis

Cover photograph by Elizabeth Blye

Roseville Farm, Boyce, Virginia (est. circa 1887)

Permission by owners: Dr. and Mrs. Eric Myer

Avid Readers Publishing Group
Lakewood, California

Roseville's Blooming Lilly

Avid Readers Publishing Group

http://www.avidreaderspg.com

ISBN-13: 978-1-61286-323-8

Printed in the United States

Acknowledgements

Many thanks to:

Catherine Owens for proofreading this novel.

Elizabeth Blye for her suggestions and photography.

Anica Moran for her good nature and willingness to serve as my photographic model.

Special thanks to Eric and Martha Myer, of Roseville Farm, for their ready permission to photograph their always warm and welcoming home.

Dedication

For seven (you know who you are) who put my writing on hold for about forty years. It made me older and wiser.

Chapter 1

Lilly Pierce buried her husband, Frank, in the family plot in Green Hill Cemetery next to their three-year-old son, Carroll Joseph. When CJ died two years ago it was a bright sunny day, a stark contrast to this cold and drizzly day in October. Lilly felt as cold and bleak as the weather.

Frank's death was sudden. He had gone to the barn early in the morning. While he was giving orders to the hired men, he told them he had to sit down. Frank didn't make it to the pile of straw; he just keeled over. That's the way the hired men gave Lilly the news while she was busy in the kitchen. She phoned Dr. Hawthorne and ran to the barn with thoughts swirling through her head. Maybe Frank isn't dead. How could he be? He's only thirty-eight. It's likely he's passed out and the hired men have panicked.

That wasn't the case. Dr. Hawthorne said it was a heart attack.

The funeral was private with only close family members in attendance. Lilly preferred it that way because she wasn't up to pitiful looks and insensitive questions.

Her sister, Laura, walked up beside her and took her elbow. "Lilly, your girls are riding to our house with Alex and Addie. John is bringing the buggy up for us."

Lilly looked at her older sister as if coming out of a trance. "What am I going to do, Laura? Frank took care of everything. For all of his roar and bluster, he was a good provider. I know nothing about the money or the farm business. I've lost a son and a husband and I'm thirty years old. If I sound angry, I am!"

John Richards, Laura's husband, wearing his snug ten-year-old black suit, the only suit he owned, drove up with the buggy. He left the driver's seat and helped the women into the back seat. The three rode in silence to where John and Laura lived in a tenant house on a big farm east of the town of Berryville. None of the Virginia countryside was pretty on this dismal day where the only sound heard was the grinding of the big spoke wheels of the buggy.

Chip Richards came off the porch. "I'll put the horse and buggy away, Pa."

Sounds of laughter were heard coming from inside the house. "I'll put a stop to that!" said Laura.

Lilly put a hand on her sister's arm. "No. Let them be. My girls have had enough sadness. If their cousins are lifting some of the gloom of the past few days, it's good for them."

The minute Laura and Lilly entered the room all conversation stopped. Even five-year-old Sarah Jane, who had been the center of attention singing *Mary Had a Little Lamb,* stopped in mid-note.

Addie spoke to her mother as Laura was hanging up her damp shawl. "Momma, the food is staying warm on the stove. Do you want me to put it on the table?"

Addie's husband, Alex, who was almost the same age as her mother, came to stand by his wife's side. "Addie has prepared plenty of food. I believe we should take our plates to the stove to fill them so the food doesn't get cold. We can all use a warm meal."

"I'll say grace," offered Lilly, who had removed her shawl and black, wide-brimmed felt hat.

They stood in a circle in the crowded room. Lilly held the hands of her young daughters. Beside them were John and Laura Richards, and their children: Adelaide, Charlie, Chip, Sara Jane, and Adelaide's husband, Alexander Lockwood.

Lilly spoke. "Dear Lord, this has been a trying time for all of us. Our prayer is that the future will be an easier path. We ask that Frank Pierce has been taken into your caring arms. He was a good father to Emily and Flossie and our dear little CJ. We ask you to bless this food that is a gift from your bounty. Amen."

"Amen."

Lilly and the girls were the first to fill their plates.

"Momma, Addie said we can all stay at her house for a few days if we want to," said Flossie, the younger of Lilly's two daughters.

"Say yes, Momma," chimed in Emily. "We haven't been up to their big house for a long time."

Lilly smiled at her niece. "Addie, it was kind of you to offer, but I believe we should go on home."

Disappointment showed on the girls' faces. They knew better than to nag their mother at this time.

Five adults and three children squeezed their chairs around the kitchen table. Chip and Charlie, too young for the adults and too old for the young ones, had taken their plates to sit in chairs before the crackling fire in the fireplace.

"Aunt Lilly, I suggested coming to our place for a few days because I thought some quiet time might be helpful," said Addie.

Lilly answered, "It is kind of you to ask. There is so much to do and so much I don't understand, the sooner I try to unravel whatever needs there are, the better."

Alex spoke up. "Lilly, I will gladly help you with the legal end of it. I am still a lawyer, although I closed my practice over a year ago."

"And I'll bring the boys down to see about the farm," said John. "If Frank's hired men are any good, they will have things in order. Should be pretty quiet until lambing and wool shearing."

Addie and Laura were busy clearing the table before bringing slices of apple pie to those who had finished.

Lilly's reaction was one of relief. "I know I will need help. Frank never let me get involved with the farm business. Maybe I should sell the place and move back here."

"Don't do anything hasty," cautioned Alex.

Lilly heaved a heavy sigh. "It is so disheartening."

The mood in the room was tense until Sarah Jane spoke up.

"We like to have you come, Aunt Lilly. Momma makes us clean up special and she always bakes a pie."

Laughter echoed in the room.

**

While driving her covered buggy the six miles down to Boyce in the foggy mist, Lilly wondered if she should have taken up Addie's offer to spend a few days at *Lockwood*. Perhaps it would have been good for Emily and Flossie. Lilly knew she was not good company. The responsibilities heaped upon her from Frank's passing were becoming clear.

At thirty years of age, she was a woman without any kind of training. She had nine and ten-year-old daughters to raise, a large farm to run, a wool buying business, and a big farmhouse that always needed some kind of repair. What was she going to do? She had already heard the talk, "*With Frank gone she won't be able to keep that place six months*".

They rode past *LLewellyn* and *Woodley* estates, past *Old Chapel* and on down to the village of Boyce. The farm stood off the main road, next to the Roseville Run, about a mile from the center of town. The horse-pulled buggy turned into the long drive up to the house. Setting on a knoll far back from the road, the white farmhouse she loved now looked forlorn and uninviting on this cold, drizzly, October day.

"Girls, you go in and lay a fire in the fireplace while I put the horse away."

"Why do we have to do it?" asked Emily.

"Because I have to take care of the horse and buggy," answered Lilly, keeping her temper in check.

From the tone of her voice the girls knew to do as she asked. In the past they had been prone to nag her until she changed her mind. Their usual calm and patient mother had become short-tempered since their father died. The two girls hopped out of the buggy and went into the house.

Lilly continued to the barn. She opened the wide doors to let in the light that was left from the gloomy day. The horse's stall was the closest to the entrance for which she was thankful. The darkening interior of the cavernous barn gave her an eerie feeling. She opened the stall door, then unhitched the heavy leather harness. As soon as she removed the bridle, Jack walked into his stall without urging. Lilly gave him a pat and smiled as she remembered how he got his name.

Emily and Flossie liked to recite nursery rhymes. *Jack Be Nimble* was one of their favorites. When the foal was born they dubbed him Jack. Frank had balked at the name, "not much of a name for a well-bred horse". But the girls persisted and wore him down.

Jack was wet and tired from the trip home. Maybe rubbing him down with a towel would be enough. In her heart Lilly knew it wasn't. After wiping him down, she picked up a curry comb and brush and let her mind wander as she curried the trusty horse.

She thought of Frank Pierce. Had she been in love with her husband? Probably not. Frank was a big man with a big attitude. People looked up to him because he knew what he was talking about, or convinced them he did. At age twenty-two he had established himself in the community as a prosperous farmer. He had been around sheep all his life. As a wool buyer he knew how to set the buying and selling prices so he made a reasonable profit. The local farmers were happy to let him handle the process.

Lilly, brown-haired, brown-eyed and grace-ful, was seventeen when they met and married after a six-month courtship. She was as quiet and unassuming as he was boastful. Underneath his bluster he was kind and, most of the time, considerate toward her. She determined to make a good marriage, which she had. Now, without warning, Frank Pierce is dead.

With a heavy sigh, Lilly gave Jack some hay and fresh water and forked out clean straw before she closed the big barn doors and headed to the house.

**

Laura Richards had watched her sister drive away after the funeral dinner. The thought crossed her mind that she should go down and help Lilly for a few days. The thought was fleeting. Lilly will have to figure things out for herself just as Laura always had to do.

Besides, wasn't Lilly better off? Laura still had two teenaged boys and a five-year-old daughter to care for as well as her husband, John. Her days were spent cooking, cleaning and scrubbing and all that other mindless labor that goes along with keeping a house. The work seemed never ending.

Laura knew Lilly hired a woman to come in and help her twice a week, a luxury Laura could never afford. And today Alex and John were quick to step in and offer their services. Laura shook her head. No, she wasn't going to her sister's place. Lilly can make her own way.

Laura thought of Alex, now her son-in-law. She had been crazy about him when she was fifteen, or so she thought at the time. His family, not liking the infatuation of a young woman from a tenant house, whisked him away to a boarding school. A few months later, at sixteen, still mad at the world, Laura married John Richards when he came to work on the farm. This same farm where she, John and their children share a tenant house. And, on the place Alex Lockwood's parents owned.

Laura thought about the ironies of life. Her daughter, Addie, at twenty-three is married to Alex. That had been the gossip of the day: a noted lawyer marrying a woman of lesser means, much younger than he, and didn't her mother fancy that same man when she was young? Tsk, tsk. Laura didn't care. She stayed away from the people in town. She had pushed Addie to be a good student and her diligence had paid off. Addie is a trained secretary and bookkeeper and she can take care of herself if she has to. Her Addie would never get trapped!

John Richards came to his wife's side. "Don't be thinkin' too hard, Laura. I can see it in your eyes and the firm set of your jaw."

She placed her hand on his arm. He had a way of soothing her hurts. "I'm sorry. John. You know me too well. Do you think Lilly is going to be all right?"

"I 'spect so," he replied. "Things seem to have a way of workin' out."

**

That evening at *Lockwood* farm Addie had retired earlier than usual. In the dim light, Alex was puttering around their bedroom shuffling papers into a writing desk.

Addie was under the covers but she wasn't asleep. "Aren't you tired out from this day?" she asked.

Alex had weathered some since he decided to give up law and run the farm, but he was still svelte. He looked over at her with a compassionate smile. "It's a day I don't care to go through again."

"Do you think my Aunt Lilly is going to be able to handle her place? Maybe she should sell the farm and move into town."

He came to sit on the side of the bed. "It isn't wise to make major decisions in a case like this. You and I will both help her sort out the bookwork. Once she knows her financial condition she can begin making plans for herself and the girls." Alex took his wife's hand.

"I worry about her, Alex. She's different than my mother. Momma would take it as one more cross to bear, grit her teeth and meet the problems head on. I don't think Aunt Lilly is as strong. She is more refined and less courageous. Uncle Frank was thirty-eight, close to your age. I don't know what I would do if I lost you."

He kissed the fingers of the hand he held. "Lilly may surprise you. And, I don't plan on making my exit just yet."

Addie sighed. "I guess it's the whole unexpected mess that has made me melancholy."

Alex patted her hand and stood up. "I'll tell you what, Mrs. Lockwood. In less than one minute I'm going to jump into that bed with you and prove that I am very much alive."

She laughed. A teasing expression appeared on her attractive face. "Alexander Lockwood, you are downright shameful."

"Yes, I am." He chuckled and turned off the light.

**

In the Pierce's large white farmhouse, Emily and Flossie were fast asleep. Lilly was wide awake sitting in a rocking chair next to the warm fireplace. She would keep the girls home and let them go back to school on Monday. She wasn't sure how death affected young people and hoped the loss of the girls' father wouldn't be a prime topic of conversation at school. It most likely wouldn't be their classmates as much as the adults who were full of questions.

The firelight cast shadows around the room. Frank had always been in the house at night. Even if she was up later than he, she could hear his rhythmic snoring. Sometimes the noise was irritating but it was a comfort also. Now the house was deathly quiet except for the blades of the rocker back and forth on the wood floor. No matter how exhausted she felt sleep eluded her. Suddenly, without warning, grief overwhelmed her and uncontrolled sobbing erupted. Lilly grabbed a pillow to muffle the sobs that shook her body. The unexpected flow of mourning continued until she could cry no more. Lilly Pierce rose from the rocker and dropped onto a couch. Spent and exhausted, she fell asleep.

Chapter 2

Clayton Lockwood, younger brother of Alex, was sitting in a Washington-Old Dominion railcar heading for the Bluemont station. It was November 11, 1919, a full year after the World War I Armistice had been signed at the 11th hour, on the 11th day, of the 11th month in 1918. Clayton had served in France. The army shipped him back to America soon after the war ended, but he was ordered to stay in Washington to help tie up loose ends. Clay figured that was his reward for being educated. Some reward. He would rather have gone home.

Clay had his fill of war. The devastation and destruction he witnessed had changed him from a self-centered young man into a seasoned soldier. At twenty-four, he felt older. The sound of a toy cap pistol, rolling wheels of a heavy luggage carrier, or the clanging of a fire bell caused him to jump, duck his head and go into a crouch. Will it always be this way?

It was getting dusk when the train pulled into the station. If Herbert Marks still drove passengers into Berryville, Clay would catch a ride. Walking ten miles down the mountain did not appeal to him. No one knew he was arriving. Addie, the girl he thought would one day be his bride, was married to his brother, Alex. His mother died last year and he had word his father's mind was failing. Clayton's eldest brother, Carleton, twenty years his senior, thought California held more promise and left. There was no one to welcome Clay home.

The short, burly stationmaster greeted him. "Last train of the day. Are you gonna' wanna' ride down the mountain, soldier?"

Clay nodded. "Is Herbert Marks still running a car into Berryville?"

"He should be here pretty soon. But you never know with Herbert. His timin' ain't the best." He chuckled at his own brand of humor.

Clay stored his duffle bag out on the porch and took a seat in the small station. The straight-backed oak chairs were pushed so close together there was barely room to wiggle. He moved the end chair a few inches. Clay's brawn needed the extra room.

Less than a half-hour later he was seated with four others taking the long car from the station. Clay noticed Herbert hadn't changed in the two years he had been gone. Herbert was tall and skinny wearing the same jaunty driving cap and gray suit. A stork in man's clothing?

He shook Clay's hand. "Glad to see you back. You've done us proud."

"Thank you, Mr. Marks. I'm happy to be back."

The big car made its way down the curvy mountain road into Pine Grove, across the Shenandoah River Bridge and headed west. At the entrance to the estate where Clay lived, a mile east of the town of Berryville, he stuffed a couple of bills in Herbert's pocket because he wouldn't take any fare. Clay waved farewell to the other passengers, hoisted his duffle bag over his shoulder, and headed down the moonlit lane to the big white house he knew as home.

It was late evening when he knocked on the front door. He didn't want his presence to startle anyone who was in the house. A middle-aged, black lady answered his knock. He introduced himself.

"Yessir," she acknowledged him. "Your daddy is in his room with the woman who cares for him. My name is Faith. I cook and take care of the house."

Clay nodded. "I'll go on up and see my father, and then I could use a bite to eat."

Faith's smile was welcoming. "Yessir. You come on down when yer ready." Faith walked away toward the kitchen.

Clay went up to his room, left his bag and cap on the bed and went to his father's room two doors away. He tapped on the door.

"Oh!" The caretaker who answered his knock was short and round with gray-streaked hair and a kind face. Clay introduced himself.

"You startled me, I didn't expect to see a man. Especially one of your size." she said.

Clayton laughed. "I'm sorry I arrived unannounced. I wanted to check in with Father."

"Welcome home. I'm Frances Gray. He may not recognize you. Sometimes he's clear and other times he's in his own world. Come in."

"Mr. Lockwood. You've a visitor."

Clay was shocked when he saw how his father's health had declined. He was never a big man, now he looked withered and gray, a different man from three years ago. He was sitting in a stuffed chair.

"Who are you?" he asked as Clay came to his side.

"It's Clayton, Father. I'm home from the army."

The elder Lockwood stared hard as if trying to remember. "Been in the army? Is there a war?"

"The war is over," Clay told him.

"That's good," his father replied.

"Can I shake your hand, Father?"

"What for?"

"Just to say I'm glad to be home."

"This is my house!"

"Yes, it is," agreed Clay. He turned to Frances. "Thank you for warning me."

"Like I said, some days are good and some aren't. Your brother, Alex, drops by. Sometimes Mr. Lockwood connects."

"I wouldn't be surprised," said Clay. "I was never Father's favorite."

This homecoming wasn't quite what Clayton Lockwood expected. He went to the kitchen hoping Faith had a warm meal ready for him.

Chapter 3

Two weeks later, Lilly was gathering Frank's papers together for Alex and Addie to sift through. They were to arrive before noon.

Lilly had given Frank's clothes to the two hired men who worked on the farm. The clothes wouldn't fit the short and scrawny men but they knew someone who would be glad to get them. Perhaps they sold them to buy a jug of rotgut whiskey. Lilly didn't care. She wanted rid of the clothes.

The only possessions of Frank's she kept were two paperweights, which she would give to the girls. Frank wasn't one to have possessions unless they were useful. Lilly, on the other hand, liked china, linen, silver, decorative vases, dried flowers, and small knick-knacks to place around the house. "Waste of hard-earned money," Frank had said. Lilly reminded him that she had dried the flowers, Mr. Green had marked the milk-glass vases half-price, and the bric-a-brac had all been gifts. A snort and nod meant he had accepted her explanation.

Alex and Addie got to the house shortly after eleven. Lilly went to meet them as they drove up in Alex's 1916 Franklin touring car.

Lilly smiled at Alex while she hugged Adelaide. "I'm so pleased you're here. I have a woman helping me today. She'll make lunch."

"That will be welcome," said Addie. "We will have to leave by one-thirty. Alex has a man coming to discuss farm business. How are you and the girls doing?"

"We're managing quite well. The girls have learned to help. The hired men are here if I need a man's muscle." She grimaced. "Then again, Frank wasn't around much to help with the house duties anyway. Ah, well. Come inside. I've stacked all of the paperwork I've found."

They left the car and walked up the wooden porch steps.

"Be careful on the third step," said Lilly. "There's a loose board that needs a nail or two. I'll have one of the men take care of it."

They walked through the parlor into the dining room where various piles of papers were neatly stacked on the dining room table. "Frank had these in different piles," Lilly informed. "I left them as they were. This pile is one I made of bits and pieces he had laying around the desk."

Addie flipped through them. "It looks like Uncle Frank did a fair job of keeping things straight. Have you reviewed any of these?"

"Not a one," answered Lilly. "I have left it up to you and Alex."

Alex had been quiet to this point. "Lilly, I'll need your permission to check on accounts at the bank."

"Of course."

Alex pulled a paper from the valise he carried. "The bank will need your signature on this paper before they will allow me to look at your records. If Frank has a safety deposit box, you will need to be present to open it."

"I don't know if he had one."

"They can tell me at the bank. You will need a key. I suggest you search the desk to see if there is a small key in there. I think that would be the most likely place to find it," advised Alex. "As Frank's lawyer and executor, I have taken care of filing the will. You are the sole beneficiary. There may be a copy among these papers."

"I just can't worry about that, Alex."

Alex was kind. "I don't want you to worry. Addie and I will take this information with us. You sign the paper and I'll visit the bank before we leave. He did use the bank here in Boyce?"

Lilly nodded. "That much I do know. You go ahead and freshen up and I'll see where Maizie is with lunch."

Lunch was vegetable stew with dumplings followed by hot tea and apple cobbler.

"Your helper is a good cook," complimented Alex.

"She is," agreed Lilly. "These early November days are dreary and the sun seems to set far too early. The stew was a good choice. I'm sure she's made enough for the girls and me to have for our supper."

"Aunt Lilly, we'd like to have you and the girls come to *Lockwood* for Thanksgiving. Pa, Momma and the family will be there. I'm sure you remember Alex's brother, Clayton. He is home and discharged from the army. He has agreed to come."

Lilly was open to the offer. "The girls and I will be looking forward to the day. How is your father, Alex?"

"Not well. We have hired a local woman to assist him."

"Unfortunately, poor Clay came home to upheaval," said Addie. "Carleton is no longer here, and Clay has never been his father's favorite. As Mr. Lockwood seems to be living in the past, Clay receives the brunt of any criticism."

Alex looked at his wife. "Clay will inherit the estate. I wouldn't feel too sorry for him."

Addie didn't have to reply, her stony look was enough.

Lilly squirmed in her chair. "Would anyone care for another cup of hot tea?"

Alex cleared his throat. "That would be nice, but we have to be on our way. We will get back to you as soon as we have a chance to sort out these papers."

Alex helped Addie into her jacket before he picked up the valise with the information inside.

Addie pulled a brown knitted hat over her honey-colored hair. "Thank you for the lunch, Aunt Lilly. You're sure there isn't anything you need?"

Lilly hugged her close. "I'm fine. Thank you for the Thanksgiving invitation. I will bring a spice cake."

"You are to spend the night," ordered Adelaide.

Lilly nodded her agreement. She waved as she stood and watched them drive away.

Addie looked over at Alex. "I didn't appreciate you being short with me."

"I'm sorry if I sounded unkind."

"You did," she replied.

"I think a tad of jealousy snuck in when I wasn't looking."

Addie was not in the mood to smile at his attempt to lighten the moment. "I married you, Alex. If I wanted to marry Clay, I could have."

He glanced over at her. "It won't happen again."

"Good."

Chapter 4

Clay yawned and ruffled his dark hair as he looked at his image in the mirror. His dark eyes looked tired with little wrinkles beginning at the corners. *Bam*! Clay ducked instinctively. Faith had dropped a pile of wood on the kitchen floor and the sound thundered. Clay left the dry sink to sit on the edge of the bed. He had to get ahold of himself. The war is over. It took him a couple of minutes to stop his shaking hand before he dared to shave the three-day beard from his face.

When he finished, he heard the woman caring for his father coming up the stairs. He went to the door of his room and opened it. "How is he?"

Frances smiled. "Good morning, Mr. Lockwood. Your father slept well last night. I'm in hopes he will eat this breakfast. Will you be home today?"

"No. I'm spending the afternoon at my brother's place." He looked at the tray of food she held. "Maybe Father will have an appetite this morning. I wish I could take him with me."

The caretaker sighed. "His health declines a bit each day it seems. You go on with your plans and have a nice Thanksgiving dinner."

"What about you? Shouldn't you be spending the day with your family?"

"No family to spend it with," she replied. "Faith will prepare something tasty for us."

She opened the door to his father's room.

"Mrs. Gray, thank you for taking care of my father."

She nodded and went inside.

Should he go in and try to talk to his father? The newly discharged cavalry man wanted to talk with his father about his experiences during the war, make him understand how much he had grown from the "mama's boy" his father remembered. It was no use. Clay's presence only elicited irritation in the elderly man who had once been in charge. The man who frequently held a blank stare.

Clay was glad to be home because he loved this place where he grew up. However, it was different now. The buildings, familiar riding paths and scenery were the same, but the change was within Clay. He was no longer the carefree lad he had been when he left here over two years ago.

Alex told him he had prepared their father's will when the elder Lockwood was still in his right mind. Clay would inherit the place because Alex had his own prosperous farm and Carleton had been disinherited because he had turned his back and left. Alex was handling the farm affairs until Clay was ready to take over. Clay supposed he should be glad. He wasn't. He wanted to finish his time at the university in Charlottesville. His buddies in the army called him "the professor". He smiled to himself and wondered where they were: Squirrel, Bruiser, and Slick.

Clay went to the barn and saddled his horse. He would ride to *Lockwood*. A five-mile ride on his horse should help settle his mind, especially in the cool of this November day. Off into the fields he rode.

Lockwood was a majestic white stucco house that sat up on a hill overlooking the countryside and Blue Ridge Mountains in the distance. Tall white columns graced the front porch with stone steps leading up. Clay rode up the long lane to the back of the house. A hired man came off the back porch.

"I'll take care of your horse, sir," he said.

The man wasn't anyone Clay recognized. "Thank you. I appreciate it." He smiled to himself. The old Clay would have expected the privilege without giving the man a second thought.

The din within the interior allowed him to enter without anyone hearing him arrive. The aroma of the feast awaiting reminded him that he was hungry. Addie came into the hall from the parlor and was startled to see him standing there.

"Clay!" she exclaimed and ran to meet him. He wanted to pick her up and crush her in his big arms, but things were different now. She was his brother's wife. He put out his hand. "Hi, Addie. You look wonderful."

Addie grabbed his hand and held it to her cheek. "Oh, Clay. We are so happy you're here. Come into the dining room. You are just in time. My family is here and Aunt Lilly and her two girls."

Clay entered the dining room where Alex came and shook his hand. "Good to see you," he said.

23

"I'm glad to be here," Clay responded.

Addie was still at Clay's side. "Aunt Lilly, do you remember Alex's brother, Clay?"

Lilly turned in her chair. She offered her hand and a generous smile. "Of course. It was a few years ago. You came to visit Addie when she cared for the girls."

Clay smiled as he recalled the time. "Your girls were enjoyable," he said. "Mrs. Pierce, I am sorry to hear of the losses of your son and your husband."

"Life doesn't always hand us the best times. I am sure your experiences during the war were not ones you care to recall. But, enough of this talk. Today is a wonderful day and we all have many blessings to count."

John and Laura Richards came to greet Clay. Then Lilly's girls, who acted shy.

Flossie spoke, "I remember you, Mr. Clay. You took us to the store and bought us pop."

"And Mr. Green gave us popcorn," added Emily.

Clay grinned. "You remember well. You young ladies are just as pretty as you were that day." He placed a finger to his lips contemplating the two. "Hmm, maybe even prettier."

This made them giggle.

Addie said, "Clay, I have seated you next to Aunt Lilly. Everyone else has found their place cards. The meal is ready to be served once someone has said grace."

To everyone's surprise, it was Alex who offered. "I believe that as the man of the house, and because we all have much to be thankful for, that I should offer the thanks."

The suggestion was welcomed by everyone.

The feast was served with the primary meat of wild turkey.

"Did you shoot this bird, Alex?" asked Clay.

"Not on your life, I'm not handy as a marksman. The honor goes to Addie's brother, Charlie."

Charlie spoke up. "I bet you're handy with a gun, Clay. Bein' in the war an' all."

"I learned to respect them," Clay replied and changed the subject. "This is a feast for a king," he said.

Clay felt rejuvenated by the time he was preparing to leave. Lilly had extended an invitation for him to visit, and the awkwardness he felt with Addie when he arrived had dissolved. After a brotherly conversation with Alex, Clay knew he could count on him if the need arose. Things were looking up.

Chapter 5

"What? That can't be possible!" Lilly heard her voice crescendo. "Alex, I don't understand."

They were in the kitchen at the Pierce house.

"Aunt Lilly, please have a seat and Alex can explain." Addie pulled a chair from the table.

Lilly's knees felt like jelly. "I will have to sit down."

Alex took a seat and Addie sat next to him. She opened the valise and removed papers.

Alex pulled the information in front of him and began, "This is what happened. Frank made good money while the war was going on. Once the war was over the government cut back on their appropriations. A large part of Frank's income was buying and reselling wool. He paid the farmers the government price, the war ended, the bottom fell out of the market and he was left with a barn filled with wool to sell at reduced prices."

Lilly sat with a blank look. Alex hesitated.

"Go ahead," she said. "I'm listening."

"Frank had to borrow money from the bank, and he put this place up for collateral. The life insurance was enough to cover burial expenses but not enough to cover what he borrowed from the bank. There is enough in the bank to cover the first payment, if you are careful."

A flash of anger passed through Lilly. "Frank should have told me this. I wonder what he would have done if he hadn't dropped dead!"

"Aunt Lilly!" uttered a shocked Adelaide.

Then the unfortunate widow simmered down. "What do you suggest? I have to have a place to live."

Alex waited to be sure Lilly was understanding. "I think it is best if you can sell the wool-buying business. Frank had this area under his thumb."

"What exactly do I have to sell?"

"He owns the barn and weigh scales down by the tracks. Also the names and addresses of his sellers and buyers."

"Selling names? That doesn't sound like it is worth anything," countered Lilly.

"But it is. For someone who wants to get started in that business, he should be willing to pay a good price, enough to get you through the next few months at least."

"How long will I have to pay back to the bank?"

Alex looked over at Addie. His voice quiet, "Two years."

Lilly cupped her face with her hands. "Two years!" After a silent moment she shook her head. "I'm not sure I'm going to be able to do this."

Addie came to her aunt's side and put her hands on her shoulders. "Yes, you are. Alex and I will help you."

Lilly sighed as she patted Addie's hand. "It's just that so much has happened and every time I turn around another problem turns up."

"Addie has compiled the names for you, Lilly. I have some contacts. We can get started with getting the word out as soon as you give us permission."

A faint smile came to Lilly's strained face. "I guess I should have started the day after the funeral," she said. "Help me set a price on this information so I can sound as though I have some knowledge on the subject if anyone contacts me."

Addie returned to her chair. "Good for you. I'll go over everything we've been able to put together including what is owed, who needs to be paid, and how much money you have to work with."

Then a somber Lilly returned. "Am I going to lose this place?"

Alex was honest. "Only time will tell us the answer to that. We'll do everything we can to help you hold on."

"I guess I can't ask for more," answered Lilly. "I say we all have a cup of strong coffee before we tackle the paperwork."

With a renewed attitude, the three set to work.

Chapter 6

William Caldwell, owner of a large estate, run by his sons, Will and Andrew, heard of Frank Pierce's wool business being for sale.

At the Caldwell estate, Will and his wife, Emily, Andrew and his wife, Elizabeth, were in the senior and ailing William Caldwell's room. He was in bed propped up on pillows.

"So that blowhard wasn't as well off as he wanted everyone to think he was," said Will Caldwell.

"That isn't a charitable way to talk," cautioned Will's father. "A farm can go under anytime. Frank Pierce was a self-made man. He didn't come with the fine backing we've enjoyed. And, I'll caution you that we have to keep our noses to the grindstone so we don't end up with the same fate." Then he went into a coughing spasm.

Andrew looked over at his brother. "You should talk about someone else being a blowhard."

Emily hurried to the bedside and said in a quiet voice as she passed her husband, Will, "This kind of talk doesn't help anyone."

William Caldwell recovered from the coughing jag to a raspy voice. "The fact is Lilly Pierce has information about selling Frank's wool business which may be something we would benefit from. Andrew go over there and find out about it. Once you do we will decide if wool trading is something we wish to pursue."

"Do you think I should go along with Andrew?" questioned Elizabeth. "Mrs. Pierce may appreciate having another woman around. I don't know her but I know how I would feel if I were in her situation."

"A good thought," agreed William. "You go with your husband."

"I don't see what good that will do," grumbled Will.

Emily, who, in the past, always acquiesced to her husband's dominance, responded. "I'm sure you don't understand, Will. I agree with Elizabeth."

The short and chunky Will threw up his hands. "Whatever you decide," he said. "We aren't going to be the only ones interested in getting a rung up on buying that business."

"Then it's settled," announced the father. "Emily, you and Elizabeth help me out of this bed so I can sit by the window. Andrew go and see if you can have a reasonable discussion with your brother."

Andrew limped to the door. "With Will, that isn't always easy."

Emily and Elizabeth brought the ailing man's slippers and robe to the bed.

"Those two have always been as opposite as day and night," William Caldwell remarked after Andrew left. The little man smiled at his daughters-in-law. "How did they end up with two such lovely wives?"

The young women exchanged satisfied looks.

**

That afternoon, Josiah Bly, the Caldwell driver, was taking Andrew and Elizabeth to the Pierce place. Andrew had telephoned Lilly, who was glad to have them come. She knew of the Caldwells but had not met them personally.

It was early December and a chilly ride in the aging 1913 Packard. When they reached the Pierce home Lilly met them at the front door. Josiah took the liberty of wandering around the farm. It was too cold to sit and wait in the car.

Andrew introduced himself and his wife, Elizabeth.

"Please come in," invited Lilly. "We could sit in the parlor but I thought we might be more comfortable at the dining table to discuss business."

"Mrs. Pierce," said Elizabeth. "We are sorry to hear of your husband's passing. I can only imagine how difficult it must be for you. I knew the feeling of loneliness when Andrew was in the army."

"Thank you. I am trying to do my best. Please, come sit. Maizie will bring us hot tea. The cold of winter is setting in."

Andrew seated the women at the table where plates of cookies sat on a delicate platter atop an embroidered mat. Matching placemats and napkins were set in place on the table. Maizie brought hot tea to the visitors and Lilly.

Lilly addressed Andrew, "You are interested in Frank's wool business?"

"My father would like to have information about the extent of it, and the price you are asking for the business."

Lilly had practiced sounding knowledgeable. "My husband owned weighing scales and the storage barn located next to the tracks. I also have names of the people and companies he dealt with. The price is two thousand dollars."

Did she sound confident? She hoped so.

"The price seems a bit high," answered Andrew.

Lilly thought so too, but she replied as Alex had told her to. "The location of the storage barn next to the railroad allows you to store the wool until it is time to load it onto the railroad cars. You wouldn't have to haul it from a distance, and if you have the names of the people Frank dealt with it will save you the time and trouble of having to build clientele from the ground up."

Andrew took these facts under consideration. "Have you had other offers?" he asked.

His question put her on the spot. Lilly was not one to tell a lie. "You are the first."

A smile appeared on his handsome face. "You are an honest woman. I'll take the information to my father. Are those delicious looking cookies for eating?"

Lilly blushed. "I am so sorry. I was wrapped up in the business discussion and I forgot my manners. Please help yourself."

Maizie entered as if summoned and filled their cups with another round of hot tea.

Elizabeth had not hesitated to indulge in a cookie. "These are as good as they look."

"Thank you," replied Lilly. "I like to bake." She didn't add that was before Frank died and left her saddled with all the chores.

"Perhaps you would share the recipe with our cook. Are they difficult to make?" asked Elizabeth.

Did this young woman not know how to bake cookies?

Andrew chuckled. "I don't believe they taught the art of baking where Elizabeth went to school. And, we have a cook who rules the kitchen. No other women allowed."

Elizabeth was quick to rise to her own defense. "I had to do some cooking when I owned the hat shop. I never had the time to bake."

A thought flashed into Lilly's mind. "I didn't realize until just this minute. You owned Miss Catherine's millinery in Berryville?"

"Yes. It was my parents' doing."

A smile of empathy graced Lilly's face. "You didn't like it?"

"It was one of those hidden blessings. If it hadn't been for the hat shop, I wouldn't have met Andrew." She sent a loving smile in her husband's direction.

Andrew rose from his chair. "From business to baking to hats. I wonder which is more important. We had better be getting on, Elizabeth. Our driver is probably chilled to the bone."

Lilly had Maizie put some cookies into a paper bag for Elizabeth to take home. She handed them to her when they reached the front door. "It was very nice to meet you both."

"Mrs. Pierce, I will call you when Father reaches a decision," said Andrew.

"Do you know when that will be?"

"I'm sorry I can't give you a date. Father will have to check all the facts. He isn't one to make a quick decision. Goodbye, Mrs. Pierce."

Josiah Bly, lean and of average height, wore his sandy-colored hair to touch the collar of his plain wool jacket. He waited at the 1913 Packard car. The once elegant automobile was showing its age, but it was still Mr. Caldwell's prideful purchase. The driver held the back door open for Andrew and Elizabeth before he looked up and smiled at Lilly still standing on the front porch. "You have some good looking animals, ma'am."

"That's good to hear. Do you know about animals?" she called.

He closed the door. "Been around them most of my life. Not only the sheep. You've got some fine horses," he added.

"My knowledge of stock is limited," she confessed.

He tipped the brim of his wool cap. "I'd be happy to answer any questions, ma'am. Josiah Bly."

Lilly hurried back into the warmth of the house after she watched them drive off. The man said she had some good sheep and fine horses. Maybe she was better off than she thought.

Chapter 7

Lilly had to let the two hired hands go. She told them she might have work for them again once the lambing season started. To soothe the guilt she felt, because she knew they needed the work, she talked with a dairy farmer who put them on. It was cleaning out the mucky barn. Maybe it wasn't what they wanted but they would earn some money. Money. She hadn't worried about that when Frank was alive.

Lilly and the girls took on the chores of the farm: feeding, watering, and mucking out the barn. It was strenuous and smelly labor. They had one cow, which Lilly milked in the morning after the girls went to school and before she put supper on the table in the evening. One day she would turn the chore over to Emily.

One thing Lilly would not tolerate was the smell of the barn in the house. When Frank was alive she had a changing room built next to the kitchen and insisted he change his clothes and wash up before coming into the house. Now she and the girls used the room. They complained but she wasn't going to allow them to go to school smelling like a barn. Lilly still had a standing in the community to maintain.

It was two weeks before Christmas. Lilly was making Emily and Flossie skirts whenever she could find spare time and keep the project hidden from the two. Emily was growing out of everything she owned. Her waists were getting tight, her skirts short and both of the girls needed new shoes. Lilly had cut down one of her own waists and a skirt for Emily. New shoes were out of the question until she sold the wool business.

William Caldwell had phoned and said he would offer one thousand dollars. Alex said that wasn't enough and advised Lilly to counter at fifteen hundred. Lilly would have agreed to the thousand because she needed the money, but she trusted Alex was right. William Caldwell said he would think about it.

Lilly thought about giving up the telephone to save money. She talked herself out of that idea because the phone had become a necessity. If she needed help she could call Addie or Alex day or night. The phone made her feel she wasn't alone, and aloneness is what she felt much of the time.

That evening she and the girls finished their chores and left the barn by the side door. A scruffy-looking man was walking up the drive.

"Girls, go in and change your clothes and start on your homework."

"Who's that man coming?" asked Emily.

"I don't know," Lilly replied, but she didn't like the looks of him. "Do as I say."

Emily and Flossie went into the changing room while Lilly went through the door of the side porch, hooked it behind her and set the pail of milk she carried onto a side table.

The man came to the half-screened door. "Is your man home?" he said.

Lilly stood back from the door. He was a shabby-looking tramp with a growth of straggly beard on his dark, swarthy, skinny face. He carried a small bundle.

"My husband is in town, I expect him home soon," said the woman who didn't lie. She was unnerved by this man's presence. "What is it you want?"

"I'm lookin' for work."

"We don't have any. The hired men take care of it."

"Looks to me like you and yer girls are takin' care of it," he parried. So, he had been watching.

His remark angered Lilly. "If you are in need of food, I will give you some. Then I expect you will be on your way. Hop the next train and try your luck somewhere else. You won't find it here."

"I can use a bite," he answered, unperturbed by her stinging remark.

Lilly hurried to the kitchen, cut two slices of bread from the loaf, buttered the bread, slapped two pieces of ham between them, cut off a hunk of cheese, set aside a cookie and an apple. Quickly she wrapped the sandwich and cheese in waxed paper. She dropped the apple into a brown paper bag, thrust in the cheese and sandwich and added the cookie before taking her offering to the hobo waiting by the porch. Lilly unhooked the door, opened it enough to hand out the bag, and braced the door with her foot.

"Much obliged, ma'am," he said.

"I suggest you skedaddle on out of here before my husband gets back."

The man touched his battered hat and turned to saunter down the drive.

Lilly re-hooked the screened door and locked the kitchen door once she was sure he had gone away. There was something about him that frightened her.

The girls were sitting at the kitchen table doing their homework. "I didn't like that man," said Emily.

"He was a tramp who probably came in off a train he'd hopped. I gave him some food and sent him away," replied Lilly.

"Is he gone for good?" asked Flossie.

"Yes, he is." Lilly wasn't sure and prayed he was. "I'll fix some bacon and eggs for supper. You girls finish up. Once we're done eating it will be time for you to get ready for bed."

After the girls retired, Lilly pulled out her sewing. She needed to hem the skirts she had made so they would be ready for pressing and packaging for Christmas. She sat next to the fireplace in the quiet of the evening. *Scratch, scratch*. She looked up from her work and listened. Was someone trying to lift a window? Maybe it was a branch brushing against the pane. *Scratch, scratch*. Lilly set aside her sewing. She went to the fireplace, stepped up on the hearth and lifted Frank's shotgun from where it rested above the mantle. It was heavy but Lilly was tall and strong enough to heft it from its place.

She stood holding the unloaded gun and listened. The scratching stopped but she knew someone was out there. She saw the knob of the kitchen door handle turn slowly and quietly, a gentle push against it. The door was locked securely and wouldn't budge. Her palms were sweaty, her body rigid. She wanted to shout, "I have a gun and I will shoot." But her throat was constricted. Frozen in her spot she stood and waited. Nothing.

After some minutes Lilly sat back in her rocking chair with the gun across her lap. Frank had shown her how to put the shells in and pull back the hammer. She had never shot a gun. Maybe holding it would be enough to frighten someone away. All night long she sat alert to any sound.

When dawn arrived, Lilly looked out the windows. All seemed to be quiet. She stood the gun in a corner and washed her face with cold water. It was time to start the morning chores, but she was afraid whoever tried to get into the house may be in the barn. She hesitated to call the sheriff's office. If it was a false alarm the word would get out: *Did you hear Lilly Pierce called the sheriff's office for nothing? Silly woman.*

What she did was wait until the girls were off to school before she called Alex. Emily and Flossie questioned her about not doing their chores. She said it was a reward for doing so well in school. Another falsehood but it couldn't be helped. She didn't want the girls concerned.

Lilly watched her daughters walk down to the main road before she called Alex.

"Hello."

"Alex, this is Lilly." She told him about the man who appeared yesterday and what she feared last night. "I'm afraid he might be in the barn and I have to get out to the animals."

"Did you call the sheriff?"

"No. It could be a false alarm."

"This could be dangerous. Don't go near the barn. I'll come in a couple of hours. Your animals aren't going to perish."

Lilly hung up the receiver. A couple of hours? It was already two hours later than she usually did the chores. How aggravating. A vagrant riding the rails and upsetting her home made her mad. She pulled out the drawer of the cabinet where she knew Frank had kept ammunition. Lilly took the shotgun from the corner, loaded a shell in one barrel, unlocked the kitchen door and went toward the barn. With one arm she slid back each wide door. She saw Jack in his stall munching on hay. The barn was quiet.

"I know you're in here," she yelled. Her voice echoed around the cavernous barn. "I've got a loaded shotgun and if you aren't out of here in ten seconds, I'm going to shoot." Shoot where? She didn't even know if anyone was in there.

His voice came from the rear. "Don't shoot, lady. I needed a place to sleep and this was as good as any." The tramp of yesterday came forward trying to adjust his eyes to the light filtering in from the wide doors.

She pointed the gun at him and pulled back the hammer on one barrel. *Click.*

"I'm movin' as fast as I can. Point that thing someplace else!"

His squinty eyes were now wide open. He was as frightened as Lilly. She pulled the gun up to eye level and he ran out of the barn with Lilly right behind. He was down the drive onto the main road and disappeared from view before she relaxed. The gun was still cocked and she didn't know how to release the hammer except by pulling the trigger. The dreadful thought crossed her mind that she could have accidently shot the man. Carefully, Lilly aimed the gun in the air and pulled the trigger. *Blam!* The force of the discharge sat her on her backside on the cold ground with the gun lying next to her. Lilly Pierce burst into relieving, exhilarating laughter. She had done it!

Once she recovered she rose to her feet and hurried into the house and called Alex. "This is Lilly. There is no need to come. I've taken care of the problem."

Chapter 8

The week of Christmas arrived and still no word from William Caldwell. Emily and Flossie were excited. Lilly hitched Jack to a wagon and took the girls out into the field where they cut down a cedar tree. Emily and Flossie decorated the tree with paper rings they'd made at school and strings of popcorn. They hung a few store-bought ornaments from years past and made tinfoil stars. The sight of the decorated tree warmed the hearts of the two young girls. Lilly could not share their enthusiasm. Frank, for all his gruff, enjoyed Christmas. But, Frank was no longer here.

Lilly wrapped the skirts she had sewn, two pencils and a tablet of paper for school. She made popcorn balls, a pan of fudge and planned a turkey dinner. It would be a much different Christmas than they had ever experienced.

Christmas morning she and the girls performed the barn chores and hurried to get ready for services at the Boyce United Methodist Church. After church, the girls were to come home and open their presents.

Services were over and they were walking home when a buggy came up behind them. "Would you lovely young ladies like a ride?"

Lilly was startled and jerked her head to see who it was. "Clayton Lockwood! You caused me to jump."

"Hi, Mr. Clay," called the girls in unison.

"Can we ride, Momma?" asked Emily.

"Yes we can."

Clay hopped off the driver's seat and helped Lilly into the seat beside him. The girls got into the back. "Be careful of that box on the floor," he warned.

"What are you doing here this morning?" asked Lilly.

"Mrs. Pierce, didn't you invite me to come for a visit?"

"Of course I did. I just didn't expect to see you on Christmas morning."

When they reached the house, Clay hitched the horse to a post. Lilly had climbed down without help and the girls scrambled out of the back seat.

"We're going to open our presents, Mr. Clay. Do you want to watch?"

"I do," he replied. He lifted the box from the floor of the buggy and carried it inside.

"There isn't much to see, Clayton," Lilly apologized.

They sat in the parlor where the small gifts of pencils and paper were opened first. The girls gave a quiet thank you. Then Emily and Flossie opened the presents containing their new skirts.

"Momma, mine is such a pretty color of blue with the ruffle around the bottom," exclaimed Emily and gave her mother a kiss.

Flossie pulled the broadcloth cotton plaid skirt on over her head and swished it around for Clay to admire. "Do you like it, Mr. Clay?"

"Why, Flossie, it is as pretty as you are."

She ran and hugged him around the neck.

"Flossie!" cried her mother. "Mr. Clay is our visitor. That isn't any way to act."

"Sure it is," said Clay as he picked Flossie up and twirled her around.

"What's in that box? It looks kind of funny with all those little holes in it," said Emily.

Lilly rose from her chair. "Emily! For goodness sakes what has gotten into you girls?"

"I'm glad you asked," said Clay. "You can both open it."

Without haste they were down on their knees and each opened a flap. Inside was a puppy on a soft blanket. The sleepy-eyed pup just woke up from a nap. The girls squealed with delight. Emily lifted the pup, the color of an evening sunset, and stood him on the floor. He stretched, then ran over and licked Flossie's face.

She giggled and picked him up. "He's so soft," she remarked.

Clay looked over at Lilly. "It's a female. She isn't much now but she'll make a good watchdog for you. Alex told me about your problem with the tramp a couple of weeks ago."

Lilly uttered a soft sigh. "No problems since. I guess the puppy can stay in the barn."

Clay was uneasy. "She's from a litter on our farm. She'll make a loyal dog for you and the girls, but I'll take her back if you don't want her."

"Oh, no, Momma," implored Emily. "We need her!"

What could Lilly say? She thought of the training required, but she didn't want to disappoint her daughters. "Thank you, Clayton. We will be happy to have her." Lilly took a closer look. "How old is she?"

"Two months."

Lilly sent a faint smile in Clay's direction. "It'll be some time before she runs anyone off."

Clay grinned. "Give her a couple of months and she'll be yapping at anyone who comes up the drive. Look at her paws. She's going to be a good size."

"You will stay for dinner, Clayton. We're having turkey." This was not a question.

"I will," he agreed.

"We have to think of a name for her," mused Flossie.

Lilly looked at her youngest daughter. "Whatever you girls decide. Please excuse me, Clayton. I need to check on the turkey in the oven. We haven't even had time for breakfast. Would you like some oatmeal and coffee?"

"Coffee," he replied.

"Girls, put the pup back in her box and come have your oatmeal."

They did as she asked before going to the kitchen.

Lilly poured Clay a cup of coffee while the girls took a seat each side of him. Then Lilly gave them each a bowl of oatmeal and poured coffee for herself. She sat opposite Clay.

"Alex and Addie say you've changed since you've returned from the service."

His big hands were wrapped around the warm cup. "I hope for the better. War has a way of making you look at things differently. I took life for granted when I was growing up. I lacked for nothing and got whatever I asked for."

Lilly sighed. "I can understand some of that. Since Frank has passed I realize that I didn't appreciate him as much as I should have. I let the hired men go and the girls and I have been keeping the farm going. I can see how difficult it must have been for him."

"Don't feel guilty about it, Mrs. Pierce. The only thing to do is to forge ahead and do what you think is right."

"What does our puppy eat?" asked Flossie.

"I believe she would love to have some of that oatmeal you aren't going to finish," he replied.

"Let Mr. Clay and I drink our coffee and we will fix up a nice place for the puppy to live. Put the oatmeal in that little tin bowl on the side porch and see if the pup will eat it."

The girls were happy and left the table to go in and fuss with their gift from Clay.

Lilly was sincere when she said in a quiet voice, "Perhaps I shouldn't say this, but I feel that I must. I need an answer. You know I am fond of Adelaide and only want what is best for her. Clayton, I also know you had deep feelings for her. Has Addie marrying Alex caused a rift between two brothers?"

Clay sat and thought before he answered. "I was sorely disappointed with her decision. Although, I will say Addie never led me on. I didn't know Alex that well because of the years between us. Knowing Addie, and after what I have learned about myself, that I was less mature than she, I believe Alex is a better choice for a husband than I would have been."

A wan smile appeared on Lilly's face. "Addie's decision took some understanding. I believe it was the right one for her. I hope things fall in place for you. With your father ill and the responsibility of the farm, it won't be easy for you."

There was a commotion outside the house and the girls came running in from the parlor.

"Momma, that yellow car is coming up to the house."

"Yellow Car?" Lilly was puzzled. Then she remembered. "The Caldwell car!"

Shortly after, there was a knock on the side porch door. Lilly went to answer. Through the half-screened door she saw Josiah Bly holding a big box.

"Mr. Bly," she acknowledged.

"Good morning, Mrs. Pierce. The Caldwells asked that I bring this over to you."

"What is it?" she questioned.

"I don't know, but it is a bit heavy."

Lilly hurried to unhook the door. "I am sorry. Come right in. You can set the box on the kitchen table."

He entered the kitchen. Clay nodded to him while he moved the coffee cups so Josiah could set down the big package.

Lilly introduced the two.

Josiah removed his cap and shook Clay's hand. He was a hired man, but he had brought the box, and he was in the kitchen, and they were having coffee.

"Would you care for a cup of coffee, Mr. Bly?"

His smile was pleasant. "I would."

The two men sat opposite each other. Lilly poured fresh coffee for her and Clay and placed a mug in front of Josiah. She sat at the front end of the table between the two. There was an awkward silence.

Lilly cleared her throat. "Clayton has recently returned from spending time in the service of our country."

"Is that so?" said Josiah.

"Yes," Clay answered. "I spent time in France and last year I was assigned to Washington."

"I was with the marines in France. Maybe we ran across or over each other and didn't know it."

Clay laughed. "That's possible."

"I suppose I should see what's in that box," said Lilly.

The girls hurried to the kitchen with their new puppy. "Look what Mr. Clay brought us," said Emily.

Josiah petted the puppy. "What's her name?"

"We're still thinking about it," said Flossie.

Lilly addressed the girls. "Do you two want to help me open this large package Mr. Bly brought over?"

"It's Josiah, Mrs. Pierce." He looked up and smiled. When he did she saw the clear blue of his eyes once again. They were kind eyes. The two men were opposite in their coloring, and in their age, height and build. Few men were as tall and robust as Clay.

The girls had not hesitated to open the box. Inside they found flour, lard, eggs, sour cream, butter, and strawberry jam. There was a note: *Dear Mrs. Pierce, Thank you for your hospitality. The delicious cookies you sent home with us were eagerly devoured. Merry Christmas, Andrew and Elizabeth Caldwell.*

"How thoughtful," Lilly said. "Thank you for bringing this over. You must stay and have turkey dinner with us, unless you have family waiting for your return."

"No ma'am. I have no family around here. It's kind of you to ask. I'd like to stay for dinner."

Emily looked at the bag of flour. "Look, Momma, the picture of the lady on the flour bag has the same color hair as our new puppy."

Lilly looked at the flour sack which read: *Queen of Hearts Flour from the Clarke Milling Company, Berryville, Virginia.* The picture of the regal lady on the bag did, indeed, have the same reddish tint to her hair as the dog.

"Let's call our puppy Queen!" said an excited Flossie.

"That's not a good name for her," Emily chided.

Lilly stepped between the two and put up her hand to shush them.

She addressed Josiah, "Clayton has agreed to have dinner, also."

Josiah turned to Clay. "You don't have family, either?"

Clay smiled. "None that have begged me to come for dinner."

Flossie tugged at her mother's skirt. "Momma, we need to have a name for our dog."

Lilly's reply was clipped, "Flossie! It can wait."

Clay was quick to say, "You girls come over here. I have a name. I'll whisper it to each of you and you can tell me if you like it."

Lilly went to the stove and the girls gathered next to Clay. He whispered the name to each of them. They smiled and shook their heads. "You can tell your momma," he encouraged.

"Momma, her name is Ef," informed Flossie.

Lilly turned with a questioning look. "Ef?"

"E for Emily and f for Flossie," explained Emily. "Do you like it?"

"I think it suits her fine," said their mother. "Thank you, Clayton."

The girls danced back to the parlor to try the new name on their dozing pup.

"Mrs. Pierce, how long before we eat?" asked Josiah.

She turned from the stove. "I am planning on two o'clock. It will be over an hour."

"Do you mind if I go and check out your animals?"

She had no objection. "Not at all."

"Want to come with me, Clay?"

"That I do. I imagine the lady of the house would prefer to have us out of the kitchen."

Lilly stood at the sink and watched them go. How good it was to have a man's presence in the house. Was it only two months ago Frank died? It seemed forever.

Emily and Flossie helped set the dining room table that Lilly had covered with a linen tablecloth, two crystal candlesticks holding green wax candles, and the small milk glass vase with dried flowers. She had tied a red ribbon around the vase and placed sprigs of boxwood on either side to make it look more like Christmas.

When the food was ready, Emily went out to tell the men the feast was waiting. They washed up in the changing room before coming to the table.

Lilly said grace, thanking the Lord for the visitors, the new puppy, the gifts from the Caldwells and the food.

"Did you know you will have three foals arriving in a few months?" said Josiah.

Lilly looked over at him. "No, I didn't. Are you sure?"

"I've never been wrong," he replied.

"What am I supposed to do with them?"

Clay smiled. "They aren't here yet. Did your husband keep a record of the sires? If they are known to be good stock the new foals might be worth a good sum."

"I gave all of the papers I found to Alex. He hasn't said anything about the animals. I believe it has taken more time than he thought to help with financial matters."

Josiah spoke up. "Mrs. Pierce, I would recommend you find the information. You will also have the lambing season starting in a couple of months and you will need the parentage of the lambs. Will your hired men be here to help?"

Lilly felt flustered. Sires, parentage? She had never been involved in this kind of talk, especially with men, and ones she didn't know well. She answered, "I will pass the word to Alex."

"I'll talk with him if that will help," offered Clay.

"Oh, Clayton, will you? I would appreciate it," said a relieved Lilly. "Now, I believe it is time for dessert and tea. I have pumpkin pie and baked apples."

Clay passed a hand over his full tummy. "I've a bit of room for pumpkin pie," he announced.

"And, what about you, Josiah?" It was the first time she had used his given name.

A pleasing smile graced his face. "I'll have the baked apple," he answered.

Once dinner was through Clay announced that he would be on his way. He wasn't fond of driving the buggy in the dark and there was a six-mile ride ahead of him. Lilly handed him a small box containing leftovers and a piece of pie. "A snack before bed."

Clay grinned.

Josiah said he would be leaving also. Lilly handed him the same kind of filled box to carry home.

A shy look appeared on his chiseled features. "Mrs. Pierce, we've fed and watered the animals, and there's a pail of milk on the table on the side porch. You've done enough work for one day. Thank you for making my Christmas a happy one."

"I agree," said Clay. "Dinner and the company were excellent."

Lilly was overcome. She swallowed the lump in her throat and stymied tears before they surfaced. "I can't thank you enough." She thought her voice sounded faint and tight and hoped they didn't notice.

She and the girls watched them go, Clay in the buggy and Josiah in the Packard. Truly this had been an unexpected and memorable Christmas.

Lilly fixed a bed with an old quilt for Ef and put it next to the warm fireplace. She couldn't help but smile at the lovable little pup.

Upstairs, the girls were both asleep when she went to kiss them goodnight. The tired mother looked down on her daughters. Emily had Lilly's coloring with brown hair and brown eyes but a stockier build like Frank. Across, in the other bed was Flossie with curly blonde hair and blue eyes and slender like her mother.

Parentage, thought Lilly. It was something she had never thought about. But, from the way Clay and Josiah talked, she assumed she was going to find out.

Lilly put on her nightgown and crawled into the empty bed she had once shared with her husband. The sheets were cold. She said a silent prayer thanking God for his blessings and wiped a tear from her eye. It is so hard to be alone.

Chapter 9

Lilly had not heard from the Caldwells as to their decision about buying the wool business. She had enough money for the first mortgage payment to the bank but her funds were getting scarce even though she had been as frugal as she knew how to be.

There had been a couple other inquiries into buying the business. Either they couldn't get the capital or just weren't interested, she didn't know. Obviously, they hadn't pursued the matter.

Lilly wondered if she should call William Caldwell. Alex advised her to give him more time. How much time? Maybe she should take the thousand that was offered and forget that Alex told her to hold out for at least twelve hundred. She was beginning to worry, which was a feeling she was experiencing too often. Lilly didn't like it.

At the kitchen table with the bills before her, Lilly silently criticized Frank for not involving her with running the farm or handling money. Her job was in the house as wife and mother and to make the appearance of a respectable family. Then she criticized herself for not having enough gumption to insist that she be included in the affairs of the place. Well, that will never happen again, Lilly determined.

It may have been Providence or plain luck when the telephone rang as she was sorting out money matters.

"Hello."

"Mrs. Pierce?"

"Yes."

"This is Andrew Caldwell. I'm calling for my father. He would like to have me come over to your place and discuss a new proposal for the wool venture."

Lilly hesitated before she asked, "Is this a new offer?"

"It is."

An inner sigh of relief and a businesslike tone, "I will consider another offer. When do you want to come by?"

"This afternoon."

"I will be here."

"Thank you, Mrs. Pierce. I will arrive around one o'clock."

"It will be nice to see you again," she said and hung up the receiver.

Her hands were shaking and she had to sit down. Alex told her that twelve hundred was as low as she could accept. What if the offer is for eleven hundred? Should she call Alex?

There was no use sitting at the table. Lilly put Ef on a leash to take her outside in the cold January air for a quick run. Emily and Flossie thought the name Ef suited the little pup better than Queen. Lilly couldn't help but smile at the chestnut-red puppy that had been a Christmas gift from Clayton. The puppy was turning out to be a loving companion to fill some of the void Lilly felt each day. Ef bounced around wagging her tail as she waited at the door.

When they returned from the brisk respite, Lilly washed her face and hands and looked in the mirror. She put red chapped hands to her hair to make it more presentable and cringed at the sight. She had always taken care of her slender hands. Gloves kept callouses away but the toil of the days' labors took their toll. Lilly placed her fingers to her cheeks and peered closely into the mirror. Where was the soft, rosy glow of her complexion? Was she beginning to look like her sister, Laura, worn down by the work and cares of the day? Was she becoming soured on life as Laura always seemed to be? It would be easy to become downcast. She looked at her image again and vowed she could not let that happen.

When Andrew Caldwell arrived in the old Packard driven by Josiah Bly, Lilly was composed and ready. She waited on the long front porch and called to the driver, "Josiah, you are welcome to go to the barn and check the animals if you would like."

He nodded and smiled as he opened the back door of the auto for his passenger to alight.

Andrew emerged and placed a warm jacket over his shoulders without Josiah's help. He reached back into the car and hooked a handsome cane over his arm. The war had left its physical mark but there did not appear to be any emotional scars. Elizabeth had hinted there were difficult times before Andrew resolved the fact that he would always walk with a limp. His auburn hair, green eyes and ready smile far outweighed the slight handicap left by flying shrapnel.

"Come right in," invited Lilly. "That January wind is biting."

"It is that," he responded and removed his cap as he entered the house.

She led him through the parlor and into the dining room. "You have a choice of hot tea or hot cocoa."

"That's very kind. I will opt for the cocoa. And, do I spot some of your tasty sour cream cookies waiting to be devoured?"

"Help yourself. How is Elizabeth?" Lilly had the cocoa in a crockery pot on the buffet. She poured a cup for each of them.

"She's fine. She is helping Emily teach in the makeshift school house. Our Matthew is four and he goes along with her. Elizabeth says she thinks Matthew is catching on better than some of the adults." His disarming smile appeared. "You realize that is a mother talking."

Lilly laughed. "We mothers have a tendency to think our children are brighter than others."

Andrew took a cookie and stirred his cocoa. "I will give you the information you are probably eager to hear."

Lilly paid close attention as Andrew unfolded a piece of paper. "Father has changed the amount he offers to twelve hundred."

Lilly looked at the paper and surprised herself by saying, "I was hoping for fifteen hundred."

Andrew sat for a moment. "Are you turning this down?"

Lilly looked up from the paper. "It is a better offer, but I'm afraid I can't accept that amount."

"What if we said we didn't need the names of the people your husband dealt with? Would you accept it then?"

This was a proposition she hadn't thought about. She shook her head. "No. The names would be of no use to me."

Andrew sighed and finished his cocoa. He drew another paper from his pocket. "Father said that might be the case, so he said he will go up to fourteen hundred but no further."

It was all Lilly could do to hold her delighted smile. She hesitated just long enough to sound casual. "I believe that is a fair price. I will have Alex draw up a contract. Would you like to have him bring it to your father?"

"That will be satisfactory." Lilly spotted a relaxation in Andrew's demeanor. "Mrs. Pierce, my father said, 'if she's anything like Frank, she'll drive a hard bargain'."

Lilly smiled. "Business is new to me. I'm learning."

He chuckled. "I'd say you are doing quite well."

Josiah was waiting at the car when Andrew was leaving. He called to Lilly, "Mrs. Pierce, you will have to have your hired men get some lambing pens ready."

"I will do that."

To Andrew, she called, "I will phone Alex to see if he can drop the contract by on Thursday."

"If he comes at noon, we'll see he gets lunch."

"Knowing Alex, I believe he won't turn down an offer like that."

Lilly waved as the Packard made its way down the long drive.

She closed the door and breathed a heavy sigh before she danced her way to the kitchen. She had done it! It was a bold move to turn down the offer of twelve hundred. What if Andrew had withdrawn both offers at that point? She didn't want to think about that possibility. Lilly would be financially safe for another few months.

Chapter 10

"Fourteen hundred!" said an astonished Alex.

"Yes," answered Lilly. "I was more than surprised. I would like to have you draw up a contract and present it to Mr. Caldwell at noon on Thursday."

She heard Alex cover the mouthpiece of the telephone and muffled voices in the background. "That's fine. Addie can type up a document. I'm aware of what the business consists of so it will be no problem. Addie would like to come and visit with you while I take care of the contract."

"Tell Addie I will have lunch and we can catch up on any news."

Alex laughed. "That sounds like a ladies lunch to me. We'll be there on Thursday."

Lilly felt as though a weight had been lifted when she hung up the receiver. How fortunate she was to have the knowledge of Alex and Adelaide in the family. What would she do without their help?

While she was basking in her good fortune, Lilly remembered that Josiah had said she needed to get lambing pens ready. When Alex makes the final arrangements with Mr. Caldwell, she can afford to pay help. Her former hired men were still working at the dairy farm. Frank had said they weren't the most dependable sort, and that he had to keep a watchful eye on their work. Perhaps she should look for others.

That evening at the dinner table Lilly told the girls that Addie was coming to visit on Thursday while Alex took care of some business. "If all goes well, next week we will take a trip into Berryville and buy new shoes for each of you."

"Yea!" exclaimed Emily. "These shoes hurt my feet."

"Can we visit Aunt Laura and take Ef with us?" asked Flossie.

"Let's not plan anything yet," replied their mother. "It is something to look forward to."

Emily was hopeful. "What about when Addie comes? Can we stay home from school?"

"The word is may," said Lilly. "May we visit Aunt Laura, and may we stay home from school. The answers are: yes, we may visit Aunt Laura, and, no, you may not stay home from school."

"That's not fair," complained Emily.

"Life isn't fair," Lilly said. "Now it is time for homework followed by bedtime."

"All we do is work," grumbled Emily.

Lilly did not correct her child. She felt the same way.

**

As expected, Alex drove his Franklin car up the long drive to Lilly's house shortly after eleven on Thursday morning. He pulled to the back of the farmhouse. Addie hopped out of the car and hurried to where her aunt was waiting at the back door.

Lilly welcomed Addie with a big hug. "You get right into this warm kitchen."

"Gladly," replied Addie.

"Hello, Alex," said Lilly. "It is kind of you to help me out. I don't know how I would have managed without your guidance."

He greeted her with a sly smile. "You seem to have done fine by yourself. How did you get Caldwell to agree to fourteen hundred? Twelve would have been a fair price."

"Andrew offered twelve. I don't know why I didn't jump on the offer, but I didn't. It was after he left the notion came to me that he could have refused, put on his hat, and left."

"Someone was smiling down on you, Aunt Lilly."

"You're right, Addie. Would both of you like a cup of tea or coffee to warm you up?"

Alex had taken papers from the valise he carried. "Not for me. I need to have you sign these papers. Then I can go finish this business with Mr. Caldwell."

Lilly smiled at him. "Andrew said if you were there at noon, you could join them for lunch."

"That's an invitation I won't refuse. It will give you and Addie time to catch up."

Alex helped Addie out of her coat and hung it on a peg.

Addie went to the stove, picked up the tea-kettle and went to the sink to pump water into it. "Aunt Lilly. The water will be ready after you and Alex are through."

Alex spread the papers on the table and explained them to Lilly. When he finished, he said, "If this is satisfactory to you, all I need is your signature."

"This makes me nervous." She dipped the pen into the inkwell and wrote, *Lilly Pierce*.

"Think of the money you will put in the bank," said Addie.

Lilly sat back in her chair with a sigh. "I have. I am going to take the girls into Berryville next Saturday and buy them each a pair of shoes and a new dress."

Addie grinned from ear to ear. "They will be excited."

"They know about the shoes but not the dresses. I want to visit your mother and they can play with Sarah Jane. Do you think you can get word to her? I know Laura would want to know before we spring a surprise visit. I'd write but the letter wouldn't reach her in time."

Alex was reviewing his papers once more before placing them back into his valise. "We can stop and tell Laura on our way back home."

"Thank you. You telephone me if Laura has other plans," Lilly replied.

Alex closed the hasps on the valise. He put on his coat and kissed Addie on the cheek. "I'll be back carrying the goods as soon as I can."

The former lawyer, turned gentleman farmer, was out the door and they heard the Franklin car rattle off down the drive.

"Addie, you pour the tea while I prepare our lunch," said Lilly. "We're having vegetable soup. There are roast beef sandwiches out on the table on the side porch."

Addie brought the plate of sandwiches to the table. "Tell me honestly, Aunt Lilly. How are things going for you?"

Lilly stood at the stove warming the soup. "I need the money, Adelaide. It will get me through the next few months. I had to let the hired men go. Now, Josiah Bly, who drives for the Caldwells, says I need to put up lambing pens. I don't know how much that will cost, or if I can get the hired men back to work for me."

Addie poured tea then took a seat at the table. "Maybe Pa can send Charlie and Chip down to help."

"I'm not going to ask. Your father and the boys have enough to do working for Clayton. It's my concern and I will have to work it out."

"You sound like Momma," said Addie.

"I finally better understand your mother. I am learning the trials of hard work. I think I took my easier life for granted." Lilly continued, "Speaking of Clayton, he gave us a present of a puppy for Christmas. We were so happy and surprised to see him. I put Ef upstairs so she wouldn't disrupt your arrival. I'll bring her down after we eat. She's a peppy little thing."

Addie smiled. "Ef? That's a strange name."

"Clayton suggested it. E for Emily and f for Flossie. It is the spelling of the letter f."

Addie grinned. "You sound like a teacher. Clay has always been thoughtful."

Lilly came to the table with the pot of soup. She began to ladle it into their bowls. "Do you see Clayton often?"

"No. He calls Alex on the phone with farm questions, but he hasn't been to the house since Thanksgiving."

"Can you blame him, Addie? He was quite fond of you. It is probably easier to stay away."

Addie was quick to defend herself. "If he's brooding, he needs to get over it. Clay knew how I felt."

"I know, but it isn't that easy to turn off feelings."

Lilly took a seat at the table across from Adelaide. "He is such a nice young man, I pray life is good to him." She sighed. "Enough of that talk. I'll say grace."

After offering up thanks, she and Addie began to eat their lunch.

"How are things at the farm, Addie?"

"Doing very well. Those Hereford/Angus cattle Alex invested in are paying off. I was skeptical when he first bought them. It's been two years." She laughed. "He's like an expectant father waiting for them to deliver their calves this spring."

"Josiah says I will have foals and lambs in a few months."

Addie held a spoon of soup to her mouth and looked up under hooded lids. "Who is this Josiah?"

"I thought I said he drives for the Caldwells."

"Yes," said Addie, "but what has he got to do with telling you about your animals?"

Lilly chuckled. "That's a long story."

"I've got time," said a curious Addie.

Lilly told her about the driver having to wait when Andrew visited, twice. She told her that the driver couldn't very well sit in a cold car all that time so he roamed around the farm. Then Lilly added that Josiah and Clay spent Christmas with her and the girls, and how they had taken care of the animals for her that day.

Addie sat with rapt attention. When Lilly finished, she said, "I hope the story didn't get out that you entertained two men for Christmas. Especially with Uncle Frank only making his demise three months ago."

"Adelaide! You can be snippety at times."

Addie shrugged her shoulders. "You know how tales get spread. Why don't you hire this Josiah? It sounds as though he knows animals."

"He drives for the Caldwells. I couldn't ask him to leave their employ. Besides, don't you think working as a hired man would be a step down?"

Addie thought about it. "It might be. What if your hired men don't come back? Spring will be here before we know it and then it will be too late. You're going to need the help. It wouldn't hurt to ask him."

Lilly wasn't sure. "That wouldn't be fair to the Caldwells."

Addie was blunt. "Aunt Lilly, if I have learned one thing, it is that you have to watch out for yourself. In your case, Uncle Frank isn't around anymore to run things."

Lilly sighed. "You are right."

Addie changed the subject. "Did you know that Lottie and Caleb are expecting their second child?"

"No!" exclaimed Lilly. "A new baby at your place. Imagine that. How is Lottie?"

"She's fine. Lottie used to complain that Caleb didn't spend enough time with her. Little Cal has kept her busy and now she'll be twice as busy. The baby is due in March."

Lilly offered a knowing smile. "It seems Caleb spent enough time at home."

Addie spilled the spoon of soup she was about to eat. "You do surprise me, Aunt Lilly."

"Will Lottie have help?"

"She said her mother is going to come and spend a few weeks. I want to be far away when Lottie goes into labor. When I had to help deliver Sarah Jane it scared the bejeepers out of me."

Lilly laughed aloud. "It isn't the most pleasant process, is it?"

They heard Alex's car coming up the drive. He came into the room with a wide grin. "Mrs. Pierce, I am proud to present you with a check for fourteen hundred dollars. Signed, sealed and delivered."

Lilly rushed from her chair and hugged him. "Oh, Alex. Thank you, thank you."

"It was worth it for the lunch. Mr. Caldwell is wheelchair-bound, but he still runs the place. I remember him from years ago when he and my father were friends. Lilly, he said you drove a hard bargain."

"I'm happy he recognized it."

They all laughed.

"Addie, take some of this soup home with you. I made enough for an army."

"Thank you, I will. Ella will be pleased."

"Your little maid is such a pretty girl," said Lilly.

Addie agreed. "She's eighteen. We may not have her for long. Charlie is making more and more visits to the house."

Alex nodded. "It isn't to see Addie and me."

Lilly calculated. "Charlie will be nineteen next month. Maybe it's time for them to settle down."

"I think they would do well," said Addie. "I'd like to have them on the farm, but they will probably go to work for Clay. Charlie knows that farm as well as Pa. Maybe one day he'll run it for Clay."

Alex checked the pocket watch in his vest pocket. "Time for us to be on our way."

Lilly filled a quart canning jar with soup and handed it to Addie, who had slipped into her warm coat and hat.

"You will be sure and stop by to tell Laura that the girls and I will be coming on Saturday?"

Addie answered, "We will."

Lilly watched as they drove away. She looked at the check she held. What an exhilarating feeling to know she had money. In fact, she felt so inspired, she just might pose the question of employment to Josiah Bly.

Chapter 11

When Saturday arrived, the day with the promise of new shoes, the girls were more than happy to zip through their chores and change into their Sunday dress clothes to make the trip into Berryville. The day was cold. The sky was overcast to the northeast and there was a feeling of snow in the air. Lilly was not going to disappoint her daughters. If she hurried, she might outrun a change in the weather.

"Emily, get two quilts and put them in the buggy. Flossie, put Ef on the side porch. Be sure she has food and water. Wear your mittens and your hats because it will be a cold ride. Oh, yes. Wear your galoshes."

"I thought Ef could go with us?" said Flossie.

"No. She will have to stay on the side porch."

"You said we could take her," complained Emily.

"It was a maybe, not a promise."

"It isn't fair."

Lilly felt on edge. "Don't push, Emily. Do as I say while I go hitch up Jack."

There were two inches of snow left on the ground from an earlier snowfall. Lilly tramped to the barn in her overshoes. Jack came to the half-door of his stall to greet her when she entered the barn. "Sorry, Jack. You're going to have to work today."

He whinnied as if he understood.

Lilly hoisted the heavy leather harness and, with difficulty, fashioned it over the back of the sleek black horse. She placed the bit in his mouth and settled the halter over his head, making sure his ears weren't pinned under. Lilly led the dependable horse out of the stall and backed him up to the buggy where she secured the harness. The heavy work was giving her strength. The thought crossed her mind that she might begin to look like a hefty farm woman. It was time to hire a man to do this kind of work.

The girls came to where the buggy was hitched. "Where do you want me to put the quilts?" asked Emily.

"Put them on the floor under the back seat. You two can bundle up if it gets too cold." Lilly looked into the eager faces of her nine and ten-year-old daughters. They were growing up too quickly. She gave each a kiss on the cheek. "Thank you for helping. Hop onto the back seat and we'll be on our way."

Jack was getting restless to be on the road. Lilly patted his neck in passing. "Give us a safe trip." Then she looked up at the graying sky, once again, before she climbed into the driver's spot and gave Jack the go ahead by a tap of the reins.

The six-mile trip into Berryville went smoothly. They arrived at Coyner's department store close to ten-thirty, walked up two steps, entered through the windowed door and turned to the shoe area to the right.

A male clerk came to wait on them. "Good morning."

Lilly returned his greeting. "Good morning. My daughters need new shoes. They are outgrowing the ones they are wearing."

The girls had left their overshoes in the buggy revealing their church shoes.

"New dress shoes," observed the clerk.

"Oh, goodness. I forgot they were wearing their good shoes. They need school, everyday shoes."

The man was kindly. "We have a good selection of both."

He was right about sizes but styles were slim. The girls sat as he removed their shoes and replaced them with the ones they had chosen. "Now you young ladies walk around a bit to get the feel. It wouldn't do to have them slipping up and down or pinching your toes."

Lilly wanted to be sure there was enough room for growth so she pressed her finger down on the toe area of the shoe just to be certain. The cost ranged in price from $1.45 to $5.95 a pair. They chose similar calf-skin shoes that were over the ankle, thick-soled and laced up the front. Emily chose a dark brown while Flossie liked a caramel color. Lilly felt a glow when she saw the smiles on their faces. Her hesitation was momentary. She did have the money, and they had not had many carefree days since Frank died, and she couldn't think of a good reason not to. After all, they were growing out of the shoes on their feet, so she let them select a pair of Sunday shoes, also. Both ended up with black patent leather Mary Jane's, although Emily wanted a beige pair with a one inch heel, pointed toes and tied with a ribbon over the instep.

Lilly knew better. "I agree they are pretty. The style is for older girls."

Emily started to say something until she saw Lilly raise a finger and knew to keep quiet.

While the clerk was wrapping the boxes of shoes, Lilly bought two sets of bloomers, heavy cotton stockings and union suits that would see the girls through the rest of winter. Then she bought hair ribbons and a bottle of lavender-scented cologne. The bill came to $19.35. Frank would never understand why she spent money on what he would have considered frivolity. The cologne was a present to herself. Perhaps it would restore a feminine feeling.

Lilly handed the clerk a twenty dollar bill which he placed in a cylinder along with the itemized bill and zipped it up to Mr. Coyner's office that sat on a platform off the stair landing. Mr. Coyner made the change and zipped the cylinder back on its cable to the clerk. While they waited, Lilly spied lovely patterned material on bolts behind the counter and longed to buy a few yards. She had spent enough.

"Looks like we're going to get some snow," observed the clerk as he emptied the cylinder.

"I'm hoping to return home ahead of it," Lilly replied.

He counted the change into her palm. "Got far to go?"

"We live in Boyce," she answered and dropped the change into her coin purse.

"From the looks of that sky, you'd better get a move on," he advised. He didn't tell Lilly anything she didn't know.

She snapped the purse shut. "Thank you, sir. Time to go, girls."

It would be wise to head for home after they left the store, but Lilly knew Laura would be chagrined if they didn't show up. She headed Jack east out of town. If they made Laura's house by noon, they could stay for a short visit. She tapped the horse with the reins and he picked up his pace.

The tenant house was warm. Lilly was glad they had come because Laura greeted her with a smile, and Laura wasn't one to smile often. Lilly hugged her sister and Sarah Jane, who was happy to have visitors.

"Come play dolls with me," Sarah Jane said to her cousins. "Aunt Lilly, Momma made an apple pie."

"Sarah Jane, that isn't a polite way to greet visitors," corrected Laura.

"We can't stay long," apologized Lilly. "It looks like we're in for some rough weather. I hope to get home before it hits, and the sky is more foreboding as the day goes on." Lilly placed her coat on the back of a kitchen chair. "I saw Chip when we got here. He's going to water Jack for me. The horse can use the rest before we have to start back."

"I thought maybe you wouldn't come with the weather looking bad, but I've got lunch ready. John and Chip will be in shortly."

"I can help," offered Lilly.

"Lunch is pretty much ready. Remember how Momma used to put the carrots, potatoes, onions and meat all together and shove it in the oven? That's lunch. I've sliced the bread so I just need to pour the tea."

"I'll set the table. Is Charlie going to be here?"

"He's up at Addie's." Laura turned from the sink with a dish towel thrown over her shoulder. "Lilly, that boy is lovesick. Wouldn't be surprised if he isn't married before the year is out."

Lilly smiled. "Addie thinks so, too. Did she tell you that I sold Frank's wool business?"

"She did. Alex said it wasn't her place to tell."

"That's the lawyer in him," said Lilly. "I don't care. The money will keep me going for a few more months."

"How are things going at your place? You look worn out," said the blunt Laura.

"I believe I finally understand the hard work you've put up with for years."

Laura shrugged her shoulders. "Clayton said he gave the girls a puppy from the litter here on the farm."

Lilly grinned. "He did and he spent Christmas Day with us. We were glad to have his company." A thought came to her. "I'll bet Addie told you he was there and that we had another male visitor."

Laura pulled the heavy pot from the oven. "She did. Something about a man you might hire."

"Addie was concerned that word would get out that I entertained two men. Food for gossip with Frank only being in the ground since October."

Laura turned with a frown. "It isn't like you to talk that way, Lilly."

Lilly sighed. "The work is getting me and the girls down. If I do hire a man, he's going to be a good one."

Laura didn't move. "So, what about the man Addie said you might hire?"

"That was her suggestion. His name is Josiah Bly and he works for the Caldwells, the ones who bought the wool business. He knows animals, but I hesitate to ask. I'm not sure it would be fair to his employer."

Laura turned back to the pot of vegetables. "Do what is best for you."

John and Chip came in the door.

"I could smell that food before we got here. Hi, Lilly." John gave her a welcome hug. "Chip told me you were here. Looks like weather comin'."

"That's why we have to leave right after we eat. I need to get home and get the animals taken care of. I promised the girls new shoes so we came ahead. I wasn't about to disappoint them. We've had enough of that." She reached into her purse that hung with her coat. "Before I forget. Here's a bag of candy sticks. I bought one for the girls, but they won't know until we get home." She handed the bag to Laura. "How is school, Chip?"

"A lot better than farmin'. Charlie's gone plenty and that means I have to do twice the work."

"Don't complain," said his father. "You'll be goin' off to college, find an office job, and Charlie will still be here. Hard work never hurt anybody."

Laura made a prune face.

The girls had been playing dolls with Sarah Jane before lunch. They ate with gusto and savored the apple pie. "Aunt Laura, you make the best apple pie in the whole world," said Flossie.

Laura replied, "I've had lots of practice, Flossie. I'm happy you girls and your mother came to visit."

They were happy, too. The days since Frank passed away were like drudgery from morning to night. How relaxing it felt to spend time with family and not have to cook the meal, or clean up afterwards. But, all good things come to an end. It was time for them to climb back into the buggy and head Jack south. Snow was spitting in the air.

"Lilly, maybe you and the girls had better stay here for the night," John said as he made sure Jack was hitched up tightly.

"Thank you, John. I have to get home and take care of the animals. It's better if we're home if we get a big storm. We'll hurry on."

Lilly placed a quilt across the back seat, told the girls to sit down on it. Then she laid the other across their knees. "You can wrap up tighter and pull the quilt to your faces if need be."

By the time they reached Old Chapel, the snow was thick and the wind started to pick up. Lilly didn't urge Jack at a faster pace because he had slipped a couple of times. It wasn't wise to risk an accident. The snow stung as the wind whipped it into a mass of white.

Jack was getting nervous. He twitched his tail, snorted and waggled his head. Within a mile of the house he was so anxious Lilly got off the driver's seat and took hold of his bridle before the buggy ended up in a ditch or worse.

She shouted to make herself heard over the loud wind, "I'm going to lead Jack home. We don't have much farther to go." All Lilly could see of the girls were two sets of eyes peering out from a quilt.

Lilly's hands were numb from the cold and the snow stung her face. She pulled the wool scarf from around her neck, placed it over her mouth and nose, turned up the collar of her heavy coat and tied the scarf ends together around her neck. The warmth from her breath dampened the scarf, but it was better than the sting of the driven snow. Her feet in the rubber galoshes felt like blocks of wood.

The snow was beginning to drift over the road making it more difficult to follow, and she could barely see two-feet ahead of her. Jack settled when she slipped her hand through he bridle to lead him on. It seemed the horse needed the assurance.

Chapter 12

It took almost an hour to walk that mile. Snow was piling up against the fence post but the top of the post sticking out was enough to guide the horse onto the snow-covered lane. Jack started up the long incline of the drive and stopped. Lilly was exhausted and knew he must be too. She led him to the side of the lane. The buggy would have to stay there.

Lilly had to raise her voice to be heard. "You girls grab the packages and go on to the house. I will have to unhitch the horse and take him to the barn. Emily, start a fire in the wood stove and make sure there is plenty of wood in the house for the stove and the fireplace."

Emily shouted, "What about the chores?"

"I'll take care of them," hollered her mother. "This storm isn't going to let up for a while. Flossie, you go upstairs and bring down pillows and all the blankets from the beds. There is a big down quilt in the blanket chest in my room. Bring that along with the chamber pots."

Lilly watched as the girls tromped through the snow that was above their overshoes. When she unhitched the harness, Jack took off for the safety of the barn, dragging his reins through the snow. The harness was too heavy for Lilly to carry to the barn. She lugged it to the abandoned buggy where she hoisted the wet leather up and onto the floor. She used the canvas tarp that had covered the store packages and placed it over the harness as some protection from the elements.

By the time Lilly reached the barn, her whole body felt numb. She took care of the horses with grain and hay and filled their water buckets to the brim. Jack needed a rub down. The best she could do was to towel him all over before a quick brushing.

The sheep were huddled together under the shed roof that ran the length of the barn on the south side, a blessing in disguise, as the north side of the barn was bearing the brunt of the storm. Snow was drifting. There was an ell on the barn that allowed the sheep to come in single file once she opened the gate. Lilly spread hay for the sheep and was pleased to see the water troughs full.

The cow was a different story. Lilly's hands were so unfeeling she knew she was not able to milk. She put a rope halter around the cow's neck and led her to a small shed with a six-foot overhang of the roof. The shed sat close to the house and had a stall area under the overhang. There was hay and straw inside the shed. Lilly would milk the cow later, once her hands thawed out.

Emily had a fire going in the kitchen wood stove. "Momma, you look awful," was her greeting when Lilly appeared.

"I'm freezing to the bone." She removed her coat and hat and had Flossie lay them over the wood clothes dryer next to the fireplace in the dining room.

"Do you want me to get dry clothes?" asked a concerned Flossie.

"Please. There's an old union suit, heavy socks, and a green sweater in the bureau. Bring down that plaid dress hanging on the back of the door. I've got to plunge my hands into warm water because they are stinging."

Emily was pouring tepid water from the teakettle into a basin. "Sit down, Momma."

Lilly sat before she wilted.

The water felt good as she flexed her fingers and felt them coming back to life. She didn't know how much cold it took to get frostbitten. She didn't want to know.

Flossie brought the clothes.

"Flossie, Ef needs to go out. Emily, put a couple of logs in the fireplace. Stoke up the embers if you need to. I'll get into these dry clothes."

They went to do as she asked. Lilly went into the changing room and put on the dry clothes. It was cold, but for the first time since she left Laura's place she could breathe easy.

In the kitchen, she put an arm around each girl and hugged them close. "I don't know what I would do without you two."

"Is the storm going to stop?" Flossie was the worrier.

Lilly smiled. "All storms stop eventually. For now, we will make the most of it, which means we need to prepare. The fireplace isn't going to be enough to keep us warm the way the wind is howling out there."

She saw the quilts they had used in the buggy piled on a chair."These are damp. We'll hang them in the doorway between the dining room and the kitchen. The heat from the fireplace and the stove should dry them out. We'll make one big pallet on the floor for a bed. I'll get candles from the cupboard."

"What if we can't get to the outhouse?" said Emily.

"Flossie, did you bring down the chamber pots?"

Flossie shook her head. "They're on the side porch."

"We'll use them in the dining room so we don't freeze our behinds."

The girls laughed.

"You're funny, Momma," said Flossie.

It was good they could smile; farm work was robbing them of their childhood.

Lilly had rested enough. The tingling in her feet had stopped. They felt comfortable in the heavy socks. "We had a big lunch at your Aunt Laura's so we will have toasted cheese sandwiches and tomato soup for supper. Later, you can each have a stick of candy."

The announcement was well received. "We didn't know you bought candy," said Emily.

"There are lots of things you don't know," teased Lilly.

The light bulb in the kitchen flickered. It wouldn't be long before the power lines were downed by the howling wind. She should telephone

Addie and let her know they were safe. Addie could call Clayton and he could carry the message to Laura and John. Lilly knew they would be concerned. She picked up the receiver and was met with silence. The phone lines were already down.

Lilly put a jacket over the thick green sweater she wore, tied a kerchief around her head, filled a pail with water and went to milk the cow.

As she stepped out into the blizzard conditions, two worried faces watched her leave.

Chapter 13

Lilly awoke to the cold nose of Ef nudging her face. She pushed her away without speaking because the girls were still asleep. She slipped from the warmth of the covers and stood. Her body was lame from sleeping on the floor. She stretched and twisted to get some of the kinks out.

The wood stove was down to red coals. Emily had done a good job of piling in wood. Lilly picked up two good-sized pieces, lifted a lid of the stove with a metal lid-lifter and stuffed the wood into the stove. They would eat breakfast before they went to tackle the chores.

When she tried to open the kitchen door for Ef to go out, it wouldn't budge. She looked out the window and saw snow up to the sill. Deep drifts greeted her eyes, drifts higher than she was tall. How were they going to get to the barn? They weren't going to be able to shovel all that snow.

The sun was shining, the temperature was freezing. The wind had settled into small gusts that picked up whirlwinds of snow. Cream had risen to the top of the milk and frozen. Emily and Flossie would think that was a treat.

Lilly went to the changing room where a shovel rested against the wall. Ef had to go out. She put her shoulder against the kitchen door and pushed hard. It opened enough that she could squeeze out and shovel a semi-circle so the pup had some room.

The girls woke up and ran into the dining room and the parlor from window to window to admire the grandeur of a winter wonderland.

"Oh, Momma. It's so beautiful," said an excited Flossie.

Lilly was frying bacon and eggs when they came back to the kitchen. She tried to share in their delight. "We are not going to be able to get to the barn today. The animals are all inside and they should have enough feed and water for one day. We can play games and pop popcorn."

"Hooray," said Emily.

Lilly cautioned, "We will have to shovel what we can because I will have to get out there tomorrow. The barn is going to be a mess to clean out."

They ate the eggs, bacon and warm biscuits. Lilly spooned frozen cream into two bowls and sprinkled it with sugar. "Better eat it before it melts."

While she washed the breakfast dishes, she saw her reflection in the mirror and winced. She had slept in her clothes and her hair was disheveled. Where was the Lilly of three months ago? Where were the smiling eyes, the rosy complexion, and the calm demeanor? She felt like a witch one minute and a general ordering his troops the next.

It would be a long day in the drafty kitchen, another night of sleeping on the hard floor. During the day she could keep Emily and Flossie entertained playing games of Old Maid, and Chinese checkers, and they could bake a batch of cookies. But, by tomorrow the snowbound duo would begin to pick and quarrel.

The power was out, the telephone was useless. Lilly pumped a pail of water in case the pump froze up. The snow was a blanket of quiet. How many days were they going to be cut off from the world? If crying would help she would sob her eyes out. But, what good would that do? Lilly resolved herself to take what came, whatever that would be.

Chapter 14

The next afternoon, whatever that would be, turned out to be Josiah Bly. He rode a huge work horse that pulled a toboggan. He wore a sheepskin coat and hat with flaps that covered his ears. Lilly could tell it was Josiah by the color and length of his hair and the strong way he sat the horse. She watched from the kitchen window as he came around to the back of the house. Tap, tap, tap. She opened the door.

He touched his finger to the hat he wore, nodded and smiled. "Mrs. Pierce, I came to see how you and the girls are faring."

She felt the pinched look leave her face and returned his smile. "Mr. Bly, Josiah," she corrected herself. "I can't tell you how pleased I am to see you." Emily and Flossie came to her side.

"The girls and I are fine. It's the animals I'm concerned about. I haven't been able to get to the barn in almost two days."

"I came to spend a few days in the barn, if that's all right with you. You won't need to worry about the animals. I'll stay out there and take care of them until some of this snow clears."

She was quick to answer, "Certainly it's all right with me." A thought came to her mind. "It's going to be cold out there. Are you sure you will be warm enough? What will you do for food?"

"I've packed a jug of water. And, I've got enough eats to tide me over."

"But, what about a warm meal? There isn't a stove in the barn."

"I'll be fine."

"You have to have one hot meal. Can you get in here for supper?"

He looked out at the big work horse with a half-smile. "Clyde's brought me over here. I suppose he can make a short trip from the barn."

"Good. We will expect you for supper around five o'clock. That's early, but the power is out. It's always good to see what we're eating."

He laughed and pulled out a silver pocket watch. "Five o'clock will be fine." He touched his hat and took a few steps in knee-high rubber boots to where the patient horse waited.

Josiah Bly was an answer to her silent prayer. While she inwardly smiled about her good fortune of rescue, a quick ping of conscience hit. What did Josiah think of her frowsy hair and the sloppy looking clothes she'd slept in for two nights? She felt a flush of embarrassment. Lilly needed to get cleaned up and so did the girls.

Josiah's presence gave her an uplifting burst of energy. The worry of the animals was lifted from her shoulders, and they would have a guest for supper. It was time to fold up the sleeping pallet, move the round oak table back into place, groom their hair, put on clean clothes, make a delicious chicken dinner, set the table with a white tablecloth and use Lilly's best dishes. There was a new feeling in the small kitchen that would most likely be their home for a few more days.

At five o'clock, Josiah knocked on the kitchen door. Flossie went to answer it. "Hello, Mr. Bly."

"Hello, Miss Flossie. You look mighty nice with that ribbon in your hair."

"Momma said we needed to look presentable."

"Come in, Josiah," called Lilly standing at the stove. "Emily, you may light the candles."

"I believe I smell chicken," remarked Josiah, as he hung his sheepskin coat on a peg near the door.

Lilly saw his blue eyes light up when he spied the lovely table settings. "You've gone through a lot of trouble."

"We needed to keep busy," was Lilly's reply. "Flossie, show Mr. Bly to his chair. Emily you will help me put the food on the table."

Lilly placed a big ceramic pot of chicken and dumplings on an iron trivet. Emily brought a bowl of mashed potatoes and one of carrots. Lilly said grace.

"Please pass me your plates and I will fill them. Mr. Bly's will be the first." How awkward she felt.

Josiah was kind. "This warm meal will set well on such a cold night."

Lilly filled the plates and they began to eat in earnest. They hadn't enjoyed a good meal since their lunch at Laura's.

"Are the animals all right?" asked Flossie.

"Contented as they can be," he answered. "Mrs. Pierce, I'm going to fix those lambing pens. I expect you're going to see some new lambs next month." As an afterthought he said, "What happened to the cow?"

"I put her in the shed near the house. I shoveled a narrow path to get out to milk her. There's plenty of milk. I'll give you a jug to take to the barn." Lilly looked over at him. This was as good a time as any. "I will have to hire someone to help me with this farm. Are you interested, Josiah?"

He didn't answer right away.

Emily and Flossie both looked up from their plates of food.

Lilly's face reddened. "Perhaps it was bold of me to ask."

Josiah smiled that half-smile that made one wonder what he was thinking. "Not bold. Pragmatic."

"Pragmatic?"

"You will need a man's help and I'm pleased you asked. It will only be a matter of telling the Caldwells of my decision. Andrew is perfectly capable of doing any of the driving that needs to be done, and I believe he would prefer it that way. It's the elder Mr. Caldwell who is more concerned about appearance."

Lilly cleared her throat. "Perhaps I will only need help during the lambing season."

He looked directly at her. "Mrs. Pierce. If I come to work for you, it will not be just during the lambing season."

Lilly nodded. "We will discuss the details before you return to the Caldwells," Lilly said.

"Does that mean that you're going to work for us, Mr. Bly?" asked Flossie.

"That appears to be the case," he replied.

"We won't have to go feed the animals and clean out that stinky barn?" Emily liked that possibility.

Lilly answered. "It doesn't mean you won't have to help."

Josiah looked over at Emily and winked.

"I have hot coffee, Josiah. Would you care for a cup?"

"Mrs. Pierce, that would put a cap on this delicious dinner."

"Momma made a cake," said Flossie.

Lilly was a bit flustered. She didn't want the man to think she had made it special. "It is just a spice cake. Would you like to have a piece?"

"I won't pass up a piece of spice cake."

They ate their dessert and Josiah indulged in a second cup of coffee before it was time to leave. "Mrs. Pierce, you and the girls have given me a most enjoyable evening."

Lilly didn't hesitate. "There is enough food left over for supper tomorrow night, if you don't mind eating chicken two evenings in a row."

Josiah smiled at three hopeful faces. "Spending another evening of a chicken dinner with you ladies will be my pleasure."

"We will plan on five o'clock again,"

He nodded. "Stay bundled up," he advised while buttoning his sheepskin coat. "It's going to be another cold night." Josiah closed the kitchen door behind him.

In the dining room, Lilly had hung another quilt in the doorway between that room and the parlor.

"I believe it is warm enough here in the dining room with the fireplace that we can sleep in here. I'll go upstairs to bring down our flannel nightgowns while you girls pull the cushions off the couches in the parlor and lay then on the floor in the dining room." Why didn't she think of that earlier?

The upstairs was so cold Lilly could see her breath. She carried their flannel nightgowns and clothes for tomorrow in her arms when she returned to the dining room.

Six cushions were pushed together in two rows and the down quilt thrown over them. This would not be as comfortable as a mattress, but it would prevent sleeping on the wood floor.

Emily and Flossie were asleep before Lilly changed into her nightgown in the corner next to the fireplace. She lay her tired body onto the makeshift bed. Lilly knew little about Josiah Bly; yet, she felt safe and comfortable knowing he was only a shout away. It seemed likely he would accept her offer. Lilly Pierce fell into a peaceful slumber.

Chapter 15

For three days the temperature had been above freezing melting enough snow so the girls could get to school.

Lilly gave them a warm breakfast and helped them bundle up.

"What if the snow gets down in our boots and ruins our new shoes?" asked Emily.

They heard a knock on the kitchen door.

Lilly opened it. There stood Josiah Bly.

"Mrs. Pierce." He nodded and touched a finger to his wool cap. "The buggy is back in condition. I can drive the girls over to school."

Lilly was surprised. "How did you know they were going to school?"

"Last evening, at supper, you said it was time for them to go. I took you at your word."

Wasn't that cheeky.

Emily was putting on her boots. "Momma said we have to go. I hope snow doesn't go down my boots and ruin my new shoes."

"The snow isn't that deep if you keep on the path," countered Lilly, feeling edgy.

"Why can't Mr. Bly drive us, Momma?" said Flossie.

"I didn't say he couldn't," answered her mother. "Come inside, Josiah, you're letting the cold air in."

"I'm sorry," he said, and stepped into the kitchen, closing the door.

Lilly realized how curt she must have sounded. "That was unkind of me. It would be nice of you to drive the girls to school. Have you hitched up the buggy?"

"Clyde is in the harness. We're ready when the girls are ready."

Lilly helped Emily and Flossie gather their books and the lunches she had packed in paper bags. Then she made one more overall inspection before she kissed each girl and told them to have a good day at school. A part of her wanted to go along with them.

"Mrs. Pierce, I'll be back after I drop the girls off and we can discuss your offer."

Lilly nodded approval. That was fine with her. She would have fresh coffee and fried doughnuts when he returned. That gesture may help to make up for her sharp tongue. The days cooped up in the house gave her too much time to think about money and the farm.

Not only did she have the coffee and dough-nuts for Josiah, she had brushed and fashioned her long brown hair and dabbed on the lavender-scented cologne she had bought at Coyner's. It doesn't hurt to look groomed.

The quilt still hung between the kitchen and dining room. It wasn't a big kitchen. With the warmer temperatures outdoors, and the wood stove sending its heat, there was a cozy feeling to the room as she and Josiah sat at the round oak table.

He wore clean dark pants and a blue work shirt. The blonde wavy hair that touched his shirt collar had been washed. He did have a four-day growth of trimmed beard. Lilly wondered how he could look so clean and not smell of barn odor. She kept her wondering to herself. They needed to talk business.

"Mrs. Pierce, you need to know my background before we go any further talking about me working for you."

Lilly sat across from him. "I would like to hear."

"I'm thirty-two years old. I was born in Pennsylvania and lived in the Amish community until four years ago."

Lilly tried not to gape. It did explain his appearance. "Go on," she encouraged.

"What do you know of the Amish?"

"Not much," she admitted. "I've heard they are industrious and not accepting of our way of life. Don't they speak their own language?"

He laughed. "Some German mixed in." He sipped his coffee. "The Amish way is a life unto itself. I was twenty-three when my parents insisted I marry a girl from the community."

"Insisted? Didn't you have a choice?"

"We were taught that our elders know what is best."

Lilly raised her eyebrows.

"Anyway, I married the girl they chose. She was nice enough. But…"

"But what?" Lilly was all ears.

He gave a deep sigh. "Johanna was never well. The marriage, which wasn't much of one, lasted four years."

"What happened?"

"I guess her lungs were weak. She didn't get over her last bout with a chest cold, which I think was pneumonia."

"You think." Lilly was incredulous. "What did the doctor say it was?"

"She wouldn't consent to see an English doctor, even though I tried to convince her. Women kept bringing her different herbal preparations they'd concocted but they didn't help." He stopped before he continued, "Maybe nothing would have helped. Each day she grew weaker."

Lilly felt a pang of empathy. "Josiah, I am so sorry. How terrible that must have been for you."

He rose from his chair. "Would you like more coffee?" he asked, while he poured some into his mug.

Lilly was mesmerized. She raised her cup and he filled it and placed the pot back on the stove before he returned to his seat.

He continued, "After she died, I did some deep soul-searching. There were times, even when I was married, I had been thinking of leaving the Amish ways. Once I mentioned the idea to Johanna. She thought it blasphemous. Once you leave, you cannot return. All ties are severed."

Lilly was on the edge of her chair. "You left family and friends behind?"

"The country was drawn into World War I. It was strictly forbidden to become a part of it. I felt strongly that I should do my part, so I left and joined the marines. The government bought Clyde. They were desperate for men and horses."

"How did you get him back?" Lilly wanted to know.

"When the war was over, I found out where they put the animals that survived. They kept good records. There he was looking as strong as he had before the war, so I bought him back."

"How did you get here in Virginia?"

"War is a funny thing," he said. "I was sent to guard a prisoner in the base hospital because I could speak some German. The Red Cross treated all soldiers regardless of which side they were on. Major Caldwell was recovering from wounds and we talked to pass the time. The man I was guarding was a German officer. He was in a coma and never came out of it."

"How sad," she said.

He shrugged his shoulders. "The major told me that if I needed work, he could use me on their farm."

"So you came here." Lilly sat back in her chair and crossed her arms. "Josiah, this is hard to believe."

"You can check it out with Major Caldwell. I am not in the habit of lying."

"I didn't exactly mean that you were telling me a story," she apologized.

He leaned forward. "What exactly did you mean?"

She gave a nervous laugh. "I don't know. I guess I just had to digest the information."

"The Amish are a resourceful people and taught me much. It just wasn't the life for me." He went to where he had hung his coat. "Mrs. Pierce, I need to get back to the Caldwell place. I would like to tell them that I will be working for you."

Lilly left her chair and came to where he stood. "I can't pay much, seventeen dollars a month. Your meals will be free. There is a room over the side porch that you are welcome to use. It's not heated, but I do have a cot you can put up there."

He offered a half-smile. "Shall I tell Major Caldwell you will be contacting him?"

"I will leave that avenue open at this point. When can I expect you back here?"

"It will only take me two days to settle my affairs. By the way, Clyde comes with me. Is that agreeable?"

She smiled. "I'm sure we can fit another horse in the barn."

After he left, Lilly pondered over what Josiah had said. An arranged marriage? Perhaps it wasn't any different than her parents urging her to marry Frank Pierce because he was settled and financially set.

Chapter 16

The big farmhouse was quiet with the girls at school.

"It's you and me Ef," Lilly said to the pup that was growing by the day. "Let's go out and check the barn."

The ginger-colored pup jumped about wagging her tail.

Lilly put on her barn jacket, hat and gloves before she pulled on her overshoes and clasped them shut.

Ef was antsy to get outdoors. As soon as the door opened, she shot out into the sunny winter day and romped in the snow all the way to the barn. Rivulets of water were running from the banks of snow.

Lilly opened the side door of the barn and went inside. She dreaded the mess she expected to see and smell after the animals had been housed inside for four days. Only the smell of grain and hay greeted her. The horses were in their stalls and the stalls were clean with fresh straw. She led them out, one by one, to get some exercise. She and the girls would put them in the barn when they did the evening chores.

Lilly noticed Josiah had left the gate open for the sheep so they could come and go as they wanted. Most were already outdoors. Sheep don't seem to mind the cold. She walked to the back of the big barn where she saw two gated areas. Each contained eight-ten ewes, the ones carrying lambs. There were also two smaller pens that were empty.

She spoke aloud to herself. "This must be what Josiah meant by lambing pens." They were also clean with fresh straw put down. She stood and watched the ewes. Ef was calm as she sat next to her owner. Lilly patted her head. "Can't be jumpy around the sheep, Ef. They're skitterish critters."

Lilly always liked to see spring lambs cavorting in the pasture. Many times, she had handfed those who were orphaned or one of twins that the mother ewe rejected. She had never been in the barn to help with lambing. Frank and the hired men took care of that. As she watched the sheep, she wondered what it would be like to deliver a lamb. Could she handle a problem? She had helped with the birth of babies. Surely, this couldn't be too much different.

The horses, on the other hand, are big animals. If one runs into trouble delivering a foal, what would she do? Her concern was short-lived. If all goes according to her plans, Josiah Bly will have that worry.

Before Lilly left the barn she went to Jack's stall. He had been curried and brushed and his sleek black coat shone like a mirror. "You look handsome," she said.

Jack stopped chomping hay and turned his head to look at her. He went right back to the tasty hay.

Lilly closed the barn door. It was time to bring the cow back to the barn. Josiah had cleaned that spot as well as the rest of the barn. When the girls came home they would have to help to feed and water, but it would only be for a couple of days. She knew Emily would complain. She was much like Frank. Yet, it warmed her heart to know they would get some semblance of their former life back again, the easier life they enjoyed when Frank was alive.

On her way back to the house, she thought of Josiah and what he had told her of his life. How difficult it must have been. He had called his wife, Johanna. What did she look like? Was she pretty? She must not have loved him if she wouldn't go to a doctor. Then Lilly remembered Frank didn't want her to take CJ to Dr. Hawthorne, and Lilly knew he loved his son. Perhaps both Frank and Johanna were afraid of what the doctor would tell them.

She went into the changing room and took off the barn clothes. There were clothes that needed washing. Lilly put pots of water on the stove. When the water was hot, she poured it into a ham boiler. Union suits, bloomers, and socks were thrown in. She let them soak while she prepared bread dough. Then she took a heavy stick and sloshed the clothes around before she wrung them out and rinsed them in cold water. She carried the clothes basket into the dining room and spread the wash on the wooden dryer rack next to the fireplace. Other soiled clothes would have to wait for another day.

Lilly went back to the kitchen, rubbed lanolin cream on her hands, and poured a cup of tea. She had called Addie, once the phone was back in order, to tell her all was fine and that Josiah had come to help. She also told her that he would become her hired man.

"Thank God," Addie had exclaimed. "We were so worried. We will rest easier knowing you have a man on the place."

Lilly smiled to herself. That was a pleasant thought. She had enough of sleeping with one ear open. After all, she was a woman alone with two daughters, and her experience with the tramp made her wary. There was something about Josiah that gave her a settled feeling.

Chapter 17

Two weeks later, Lilly watched Addie and Laura arrive in a smart-looking buggy with fastened side canvas flaps that gave some protection from the weather. Addie had called the week before to say they were coming.

Lilly threw a shawl around her shoulders and went out to meet them as they came to the back of the house. She hugged each of them. "You don't know how happy I am to see you. It seems like I have been cooped up in this house forever. I haven't even been able to get into town to buy groceries."

"You look rested," said Addie.

Lilly didn't respond. "Come inside. I have the water hot for tea."

They hung up their coats and warmed their hands over the wood stove.

"Alex bought that buggy because it would be warmer. It's still cold in this February air," said Addie.

Laura had been quiet. She spied the dried flowers in the milk glass vase that sat in the middle of the round oak table. "The flowers are pretty, Lilly."

"I need something to brighten these winter days. I finally took the quilt down between the dining room and kitchen, but I had to leave one up between the parlor and the dining room. The girls and I have been sleeping on a pallet in the dining room, close to the fireplace. Our upstairs rooms have frost on the walls and windows."

"I guess that's what's better about having a smaller house," said Laura. "Our fireplace is enough."

Was Laura just stating a fact or was she envious of her sister? Lilly was never quite sure how to take Laura.

"Tell me about how things are going for you," said Lilly after she'd poured the tea and taken her seat.

Addie spoke, "Alex is all excited about his cattle. He said you should think of raising some of the same. How is your hired man working out?"

"Josiah has taken a burden off my shoulders," Lilly answered. "So far, I am keeping my head above water. He will be in to pick up his lunch. You can meet him then." She turned to Laura. "How is Clayton doing?"

Laura took a sip of tea. "John says he is trying his best to keep the farm going and take care of Mr. Lockwood."

"How is his father?" asked Lilly.

"I keep my distance. John says the old man is getting worse. John has had to go over and help pick him up off the floor or help find him if he's wandered from the house."

"Wandered from the house!" said an astonished Lilly.

"That's happened a couple of times. Clayton needs a younger woman to care for his father.

106

Alex should be looking into that, Addie," said her mother.

Addie was defensive. "Alex does what he can. He can't be down there every minute."

Laura did have a way of raising hackles.

"We will have chicken noodle soup for lunch and ham and cheese sandwiches," said Lilly, as a way of easing the tension.

"I've brought some sour cream cookies Lottie made. You know how Lottie Bell likes her cookies." Addie was all smiles.

"Oh, yes. And, how is Lottie? Is her baby about due?"

"She seems to be doing well, Aunt Lilly. She says the baby should arrive in about a month."

"Everything seems to bloom in the spring," said Lilly.

There was a knock on the kitchen door.

Lilly raised her eyebrows and tilted her head. "That will be Josiah coming for his lunch."

"Does he eat in the kitchen?" said Laura.

"No, he takes it up to his room."

"His room! I hope he doesn't have a room upstairs!" said Addie.

Lilly put a finger to her lips. "I'll explain later."

Lilly answered the knock.

"Afternoon, Mrs. Pierce."

"Josiah, I have your lunch ready. First, I would like to have you meet my sister and my niece."

He did not enter the kitchen. Lilly introduced them from a distance.

He nodded to them. "Ladies, I apologize for being in my work clothes."

"No need to," said Laura. "My husband runs a farm. Work clothes are a way of life."

Josiah smiled at her. "Thank you, ma'am."

Lilly handed him his lunch of a sandwich wrapped in wax paper and a pottery mug of soup.

"Would you like to have a sour cream cookie to go with that?" asked Addie.

"I would," he answered.

Addie took a cookie from a box she had set on a chair and handed it to him.

"Thank you." He touched his cap. "It was a pleasure to meet you ladies."

After he left, Lilly took her seat at the table. "Well, what do you think?"

"His smile lights up his blue eyes," said Addie. "He's not a big man but he's tall enough and he looks strong and wiry."

"Lilly, you did embarrass him," admonished her sister.

"I didn't mean to. I wanted you to meet him; so you can rest easy."

"What about this room he has?" asked Addie.

Lilly chuckled. "It's not in the house. He's fixed up that room over the side porch."

"Adelaide, why are you so concerned about propriety," said her mother. "There were plenty of stories floating around when you married Alex."

Addie's face burned. Would her mother never let her forget that Alex is sixteen years older and had once been an infatuation of her mother's?

Lilly put lunch on the table. "I'll tell you about Josiah's background. You can draw your own conclusions."

By the time lunch was finished, they were all in a good mood. Both Laura and Addie approved of Josiah.

"Lilly, I believe I won't have to worry about my little sister anymore," said Laura. "I was concerned about you after Frank died because you have had an easier life than I've had. You are doing fine." She hugged Lilly.

Lilly returned the hug and smiled. "I'm only a few years younger than you, Laura."

"True, but you've always been my little sister." How unlike Laura.

Addie had put on her coat and gave Lilly a hug goodbye. "I am so glad we came," she said. "I believe your hired man is going to work out fine." She turned to her mother. "Ready for the cold trip home, Momma?"

Laura patted her daughter on the back. "This trip has warmed our hearts. I believe the feeling will carry us home."

Chapter 18

Josiah had put a pot-bellied stove in his room above the porch. It was enough to keep the cool of the room at a tolerable level. He told Lilly that she needn't make him breakfast anymore because he could perk his coffee and cook up some oatmeal on the stove. In return, Lilly washed his sheets and pillow cases. He left them outside the kitchen door every Monday.

Lilly had him take supper in the kitchen with her and the girls. Josiah looked forward to that. The food was always warm. If Lilly was busy cleaning up, he let the girls read to him or helped them with arithmetic problems. Lilly had asked him how he had learned. "The Amish have schools," he'd answered.

He didn't need to add that because he was a hired man didn't mean he was dumb, so he didn't. The look of chagrin on her face was enough.

Josiah liked living on the farm. It was hard work that kept him busy. It kept his mind off his twenty-year-old sister. Even though he had left the Amish way of life, he had kept in touch with her by sending her his address. He remembered Rebecca was the one appointed to fetch the mail so he trusted she would be the first to get his note. Little changed in the Amish way of life. Mail was one English way the Amish had allowed because they could keep in touch with other Amish communities in the country.

He was holding a letter from her which meant she had received his address and note that he was well. Josiah sat on the side of the cot in his room with the letter in his hand. Rebecca was in turmoil. It was past time for her to marry, according to her parents. They had picked out an older man, whose wife had died, to be her husband. Rebecca wrote she shuddered at the thought of being married to an old man she didn't like. She was afraid to defy her parents. Couldn't Josiah do something?

What could he do? Rebecca had always been his favorite. He had watched out for her since he was twelve and she was a newborn. He had held her when she cried, rocked her to sleep, taught her how to ride a horse and hitch up a buggy. How could he turn his back on her now? The letter was so disturbing he knew he wouldn't sleep. He decided to see if Lilly was still awake.

Tap, tap, tap on the kitchen door.

Lilly opened it a crack to see who was there. "Josiah! What are you doing here? The girls are asleep and I'm finishing up before I retire," she said in a hushed voice.

He spoke quietly, "I am sorry, Mrs. Pierce. I have a problem. May I come in?"

"Does it have to do with the animals?"

"Nothing so easy," he replied.

She opened the door. "Come in and have a seat."

Josiah sat at the table and Lilly sat opposite. He pulled the letter from his pocket and read it to her.

When he finished, she sat for a moment. "How awful. The poor girl must be frightened to death."

"She is asking for my help. I don't know what to do. It was easier for me to leave because I went into the service. If she leaves, she has nothing. I have nothing to offer her."

"You can't leave her there."

"What do you suggest?"

Lilly didn't hesitate. "If you can get her away, she can stay here in that room off the parlor. At least until something turns up. People are always looking for good help. She is healthy, isn't she?"

He nodded. "She is used to being industrious. If she could stay here until she found employment, it would take a big worry off my mind. She would be a help to you."

"Do you think you can get her here?"

Josiah had given that some thought. "She goes to a young people's meeting on Wednesdays. If I can intercept her on her way, we can figure out a plan."

"That means you would have to go up there."

He nodded. "I don't see any other way. It isn't safe to send her train tickets."

"If you go by train that would mean tickets for you and for her. That would be costly."

"I will go to the train station tomorrow to see what connections I can make, and how expensive it will be."

Lilly had an idea. "Alex has a car. I can call up there and see if he is agreeable to driving you to Pennsylvania."

"This is my problem."

Lilly sighed. "How long will you be gone?"

"I'm not sure. A week?"

Lilly sat back in her chair. She didn't care for the idea of having to do the barn chores. How would she feel if she were young and forced to marry an older man she didn't like? The thought wasn't pleasant. "You need to go as soon as you can."

Josiah stood. "Thank you. I hoped you would understand."

Josiah left and went up to his room.

Chapter 19

The next morning Josiah did the barn chores before he went to the railroad station to see about transportation to Paradise. The stationmaster suggested the best route was to catch the Baltimore&Ohio in Harpers Ferry, West Virginia over to Brunswick, Maryland." The stationmaster pulled out a map of intersecting railroads. "Next place to go is to Frederick, Maryland. In Frederick you'll take the same route General Lee took to Gettysburg. That'll get you in the neighborhood. Course you could go by way of Hagerstown or Philadelphia, but I wouldn't recommend it."

It would still be a distance from Gettysburg to Lancaster. "Are you sure I will be able to make connections to get me to Lancaster?"

"Oh, sure. There's railroad spurs all over the place."

Josiah thanked him. He had twenty-five dollars in savings. The amount would cover tickets and incidentals. He went back to the farm, took the stairs to his room and prepared to leave.

To his surprise, Lilly had hitched Jack to the buggy and waited at the back of the house. "Mrs. Pierce, I can walk to the station."

"Of course you can. A ride is better."

He climbed up beside her.

Lilly looked at him. "Are you sure you have enough money? I can pay you next month's wages if you need them."

He looked directly at her with a wide smile. "You are most kind. I will be fine."

Lilly tapped Jack with the reins and they headed down the drive.

"I'll return as soon as I can. You may have a couple new lambs before I get back. I've penned those ewes separately."

"I hope they wait until you get back." she said. "Do you feel secure with the information you've been given?"

He nodded. "Once I get to York, it will be in familiar territory. Not much changes."

"Be safe. You do have to be here when the horses are ready to drop their foals."

He laughed. "It's good to know I'm useful for something."

Lilly blushed. "Josiah, I don't know how I could run the farm without you. The girls and I will look forward to your return. The front room will be ready for Rebecca."

He turned and looked at her. "I promise to get back here as soon as I can."

Lilly pulled the buggy into the station yard. There was a trace of snow on the ground, but the sun was shining. "Tell me the truth, Josiah. Is there danger in this trip?"

"The only danger is that my parents will learn of Rebecca's plan to leave and will force her to stay."

"Can they do that?"

"They can. I know you and the girls can take care of things while I'm away." A half-smile appeared. "Flossie will do her best and I'm sure Emily will complain, but she is a good worker."

"You know my girls well."

"They are good girls."

They rode through the town of Boyce to the railroad tracks.

He pulled out a pocket watch. "I have another fifteen minutes. It will be a pleasure to wait in the most elegant station. I'm told they have indoor plumbing."

Lilly laughed. "Take the box on the back seat. I packed lunch for you."

He jumped out of the buggy, took the box and sniffed it. "I smell fried chicken."

"It's as good cold as it is warm," she said.

He stood for a minute. "Thank you, Mrs. Pierce."

"Hurry back." She tapped the reins for Jack to turn the buggy around. It wouldn't do for Josiah to see tears in her eyes.

Lilly hadn't realized how much she depended on this man. Just when life was getting easier, she would have to take over the barn chores, and, at night, she wouldn't feel as secure as when she knew he was in the upstairs room. Maybe she would have to deal with lambs being born. The realities were enough to make anyone cry.

Lilly had business in town. First she went to the bank to make the second payment on the loan

Frank had burdened her with. She knew the teller. "Good morning, Mr. Fisher. I'm here to pay on my loan."

"Good morning, Mrs. Pierce. I'll be happy to take care of that for you."

Lilly slid the envelope containing money and payment through the opening beneath the barred area separating the teller from her. At a side glance, she saw a lady and gentleman enter. It was Gloria Sanderson and her husband. Gloria was the biddy hen in Boyce just as Lavinia Talley was in Berryville. Lilly knew them both. She hoped Gloria didn't spot her.

"Lilly! Lilly Pierce." Gloria came bustling over. "My goodness, I thought that was you. I haven't seen you for a while. How are things going?"

"Good morning, Gloria. Things are fine."

"It must be difficult for you with Frank gone." Gloria was always the sensitive one. "I understand you have a new hired man."

"I do."

"He used to drive for the Caldwells?"

"He did."

With a coy turn of her head and a half-smile, she said, "Weren't you lucky to snare him away?"

Lilly turned to face her. "I didn't snare him. He came on his own free will."

Gloria gave a nervous laugh. "Oh, of course he did." She waited a beat to see if Lilly would offer any more information. "Well, I need to see if Ronnie is finished with his business. Bye, bye, Lilly."

"Good-bye, Gloria."

The teller slipped the empty envelope back to Lilly. "Thank you, Mrs. Pierce. It is always a pleasure to see you."

And to take my money, thought Lilly. Talking with Gloria Sanderson had been the catalyst to sour her day.

Outdoors, Lilly stood next to the front column of the bank. She needed groceries, and she needed sheets and pillowcases for the chaise in the front room where Rebecca would be staying. The spare set of bed linens had been given to Josiah. The wise move was to go to the department store first and the grocery second.

Lilly had parked the buggy across the street from the bank. She crossed the main street of Boyce and entered the two-story mercantile. The store wasn't as big as Coyner's in Berryville, but the selection of material she needed would do.

Lilly fingered the different cloths. Although she liked the percale, she decided on the cotton muslin that was less expensive at fifteen cents a yard.

"Mrs. Pierce, how nice to see you. It's been a while since you've been in."

This used to be Lilly's favorite place to browse when Frank was alive. She bought all of her sewing goods here and other variety of articles of necessity.

Lilly smiled at the clerk. "Hello, Miss Harris. The farm keeps me busy. I don't get in to town as often as I used to."

"We were all sorry to hear of your loss of Mr. Pierce."

"Thank you," Lilly replied. Miss Harris was one of the sincere people she appreciated. "I need sheeting material."

"Our finest is this percale, but I have found, if you put baking soda in the wash water, the muslin softens up and works just as well. It's a strong fiber." She pulled the material this way and that to demonstrate its strength.

"I trust your judgement," said Lilly. "They will only be utility sheets so I believe the muslin will work nicely. How wide is this?"

Miss Harris knew her material. "This comes in a thirty-two inch width. You will need to allow for some shrinkage."

Lilly did a quick calculation in her head. The chaise was six-feet long and about two-feet wide. "I'll need five yards."

Her eye caught pretty lace on a spool. Wouldn't that be lovely to trim the pillowcase? Too much. She needed the money for groceries.

Miss Harris measured out the five yards of cream-colored muslin, folded it neatly and placed it in a paper bag. "Will there be anything else?"

Lilly shook her head.

The clerk wrote a bill of sale for seventy-five cents.

Lilly pulled a dollar bill from her purse and waited for the twenty-five cents in change. That quarter would buy a dozen eggs.

It was early afternoon when she put the last of the groceries into the buggy. Mr. Green carried out the large bag of potatoes and placed it on the back seat. "Miss Lilly, I don't mean to sound out of line, but if you ever need to start a credit account just say the word."

She understood what he meant and took no offense. It isn't as easy for a woman to keep a farm going. "Thank you, Mr. Green. The time may come when I may have to take you up on that."

Lilly could see from his gratified smile that he was glad he made the offer.

She drove up the main street of Boyce and guided Jack left onto Greenway, heading for home. The sky was clouding up to the west. It didn't feel cold enough to snow. Yet, Virginia weather can change quickly. And, it is almost the end of February, and there are groceries to carry, and lambs could be coming, and Josiah isn't here... Lilly tapped the reins sending Jack into a trot.

Chapter 20

Clayton Lockwood was in his office at the house working on paperwork when he heard an urgent cry, "Mr. Clay, I need your help!"

He hurried from the room to where he saw his father's caretaker was on the stair landing trying to prevent his father from entering the stairs. Clayton bounded up the flight of stairs and took his father's scrawny arm. "Careful there. The stairs are steep."

The elderly man was scrawny but strong and combative when agitated. "Who are you? Where's Mrs. Lockwood?"

"I'm Clayton, Father. Mother isn't here."

The wild eyes of his father looked at him. He tried to wrench his arm free. "You're not Clayton. He's in the army."

Clayton held firmly lest the old man would hurtle down the stairs. "Let's go back into your room. You can wait there until Mother returns."

These words seemed to calm the confused man, and he allowed Clayton to lead him back into his room. Clayton helped him into bed where the old man sighed and drifted off to sleep. Clay motioned for Mrs. Gray to follow him.

They stood on the stair landing. "I will have to have a room prepared for him on the first floor. I thought it was better to have a room familiar to him, but in his present state, I don't think it matters."

Mrs. Gray nodded. "Mr. Clay, you and I have both seen how he is failing. I don't want to leave, but I can't handle him anymore. If you weren't here, he could have fallen down those stairs and broken his neck. I can't be responsible if he injures himself." She was shaking.

Clay knew she spoke the truth. He had been hoping Dr. Hawthorne could give some medicine that would help. The chloral hydrate helped at bedtime, but the man couldn't sleep twenty-four hours a day.

"Mrs. Gray, I understand. I'll have a room readied this afternoon and we'll move him down. I will try to find someone to replace you, if you think you need to leave. Until then, I can see someone is here at all times when you need assistance."

Mrs. Gray was in her fifties, a round, short and kind person. Clay towered over her.

She said, "The best is for you to find someone to take my place. It is better for you and for me. If you can promise someone will be here to help when I need it, I will stay until you find a replacement." She added, "You are a good employer. I will be glad to vouch for you."

Clayton had never thought of an employee vouching for an employer. It was usually the other way around. He smiled. "That's fair," he said to her. "I promise that I will be looking for someone tomorrow. It will take some time. Meanwhile, I'll see if Chip Richards can sit here in my absence."

Mrs. Gray nodded her agreement and went back to the room to sit with the elder Lockwood.

Clay went back to the paper work. His father had invested in stocks that were paying good dividends, but the farm itself wasn't showing a good enough profit. Now he had the worry of finding good help for his father. Clayton knew he should consult with Alex. It wasn't fair to shoulder this care of their father by himself. He flipped the pencil he was using into the air. It landed on the desk and rolled onto the floor. He might as well head over to the Richards' house to see if Chip is available.

Why wasn't his life turning out as he had planned? He'd had an easy life, spent three years at the university, and served two years in the military. That should serve for something other than taking care of his father and trying to run a horse farm he knew little about.

Lilly Pierce jumped into his mind. She was a lovely lady who had lost her husband and was left to care for two daughters and run a sheep farm she knew nothing about. He hadn't given that much thought before. If anyone should feel sorry for their lot in life, it should be her. He was glad he had given them the pup. Perhaps he should make a trip down there to see how things are going.

Clay put on his jacket and hat. He drove his father's Model T.

Laura Richards came to the door. She wasn't as warm and welcoming as her sister. In fact, Clay always felt constrained in her presence. He removed his hat. "Mrs. Richards is Chip at home?"

"He's out in the barn."

"We are having a dickens of a time with my father. He's getting to be too much for Mrs. Gray. I will be searching for a new caretaker. In the meantime, I wonder if Chip could fill in by being at the house if she needs help."

"How often would that be?"

"Afternoons, after lunch to supper time. It wouldn't have to be every day. Three days a week would be a great help. I'll pay him."

"He can use the money. He starts college next year." Laura didn't mince words. "I'll tell him when he comes in."

"I would be appreciative if he would come tomorrow."

"I'll see that he gets there," she said and closed the door.

Clay stood with his hat in his big hands. When one door closes another one opens. He was going to visit Lilly and the girls. They made him feel welcome. Clayton Lockwood needed to feel good about something.

Chapter 21

The next morning was heavy fog that cleared up as the morning sped by. Clay took a bath, shaved, and put on a clean shirt and pants. He anxiously awaited Chip because he wasn't sure he would show up. Right after lunch, Chip knocked on the back door. The cook went to answer it. Clay was there first.

He shook Chip's hand. "I'm glad to see you. Follow me. I'll introduce to Mrs. Gray. All you have to do is sit here in the parlor and give her a hand when she needs it."

Clay made the introduction and showed Chip the library. He was welcome to read any of the books. "I'll be back before supper."

He cranked up the Model T. The February air was cool but it had that spring feeling. He stopped at Coyner's and bought a box of Fannie Farmer chocolates. The road to Boyce was bumpy and rutty but the car was faster and warmer than being on horseback.

Clay pulled up the long drive to the Pierce house and drove around to the back. Lilly came out of the kitchen door with a wool shawl around her shoulders, Ef following at her heels. "Clayton, how happy I am to see you."

Ef was jumping around and barking.

"Quiet, Ef," Lilly was firm. "I believe she's as pleased to see you as I am. Come in. Would you like tea or coffee?"

"Good to see the pup is growing. Don't go through any bother, Mrs. Pierce. I came to see how things are going for you and the girls."

"It is no bother. Have a seat at the table while I put the kettle over for tea. Have you had lunch?"

"Yes, ma'am."

"I suppose we should sit in the dining room. Unfortunately, I have it littered with sewing materials. I'm making sheets for a chaise."

She sat opposite him. "Tell me now. What is news in Berryville?"

"I don't make it into town often. I can tell you how it is at my place."

"How is that? I haven't heard from my sister for weeks. I have to assume all is well with her and the family."

He nodded. "I saw Mrs. Richards yesterday. I have hired Chip to stay at the house in my absence. My father is doing poorly."

"I am sorry to hear that."

He sighed. "His physical health is good enough, but mentally he's in his own world. I find I am not the best at running a farm."

The whistle on the teakettle sounded. Lilly went to fix the tea.

"That makes two of us. Did you know that I have hired Josiah Bly?"

Clayton shook his head. "He should do well. Is he around?"

Lilly put two pottery mugs filled with hot water on the table and dropped a teabag into each. Mugs were easier for Clayton to handle than delicate tea cups.

She took her seat. "Josiah left two days ago. He went to Pennsylvania to get his sister. Did you know he used to be Amish?"

"No wonder he knows how to work. He isn't like many of the run-of-the-mill hired hands."

"When we finish the tea, we'll go to the barn. You can see the changes he's made. I have been going out two or three times a day to check on the ewes. He said they may lamb before he gets back. I have never had to go to the barn to help bring lambs into the world."

Clayton sipped his tea. "Isn't that a natural process?"

She shrugged her shoulder. "I suppose it is, but there is the danger of one not coming headfirst, just like with human babies. All in all, it has put me on edge."

"How are Emily and Flossie?"

"They are not happy that we have to do the barn chores while Josiah is gone. Their grades in school improved once we didn't have all of the responsibility of the animals." She stopped before she continued, "I am going to see to it they get further education. I can understand why Laura pushed Adelaide."

"Addie's mother was hard on her," said Clayton.

Lilly agreed. "But, look how Addie has turned out. I'm sure she could run *Lockwood* if something happened to Alex."

Clay grinned. "I'm sure she could."

They walked out to the barn. Clayton was impressed with the neatness of the interior and the workmanship of the lambing pens. "I believe you have found a gem in your hired man."

They stood by the smaller pens. "These are the ones I'm keeping an eye on. I hope Josiah gets back here before I run into trouble."

He turned to look at her. "What makes you think you will run into trouble?"

She chuckled. "I don't know. I guess I've had so many things go wrong, I look forward to the next one."

He gave true belly laugh. "Not much to look forward to. I understand what you mean. I not only have my father to worry about, along with the farm, but the caretaker for my father is leaving. I have to scout up another."

"Do you have anyone in mind?"

He shook his head. "A man could probably manage Father better than a woman. I had a buddy in the army, we called Slick. He worked as an orderly in the hospital when he was in the military. I have his address in New York City."

Lilly turned her head toward him and raised her eyebrows. "I can't imagine someone from the city would want to come down here. Especially someone called, Slick."

His dark eyes were filled with merriment under thick brows. "We called him that because he knew how to procure rationed goods and keep us out of trouble playing cards and dice. I don't know. Maybe he is married by now."

Lilly thought for a moment. "I suppose it wouldn't hurt to send him a note."

They walked away from the pens and out of the barn. Ef followed.

School was out and Emily and Flossie were coming up the drive. When they spied Clay they came on the run.

"Mr. Clay," hollered Emily. "What are you doing here?"

"Emily. That is no way to greet a visitor," Lilly reprimanded.

"Hello, Mr. Clay," said Flossie.

Clay bent his large frame down and put an arm around each girl. "I came to see how Ef is doing?"

"Didn't you come to see us?" said a disappointed Flossie.

"Of course I did. I brought you and your mother a present from Mr. Coyner's store."

That made their eyes widen even more when he pulled out the box of Fannie Farmer chocolates, tied with a lace ribbon. The silhouette of a woman was etched into the tin.

"Can you come in and play a game of Chinese checkers? Mr. Bly plays with us sometimes," said Emily. "He's gone to get his sister, Rebecca, but he'll be back."

"Will she be staying here?" he asked Lilly.

Lilly nodded. "I will tell you the story another time."

Clay went into the house with them. The girls put their books away and brought the game of checkers to the kitchen table. Lilly was busy peeling potatoes for their evening meal.

They finished the game in a half-hour amid shouts of joy and disappointment before Clay announced that it was time for him to leave. "I apologize for not phoning before I came," he said to Lilly. "I had to get out of the house. If you weren't here, the ride would have done me good."

"Your visit has brightened our day, Clayton. Thank you for the chocolates; we will savor them. You are welcome any time."

"I appreciate your kindness, Mrs. Pierce. I hope your hired man gets back here soon."

Lilly placed the shawl over her shoulders and walked him to the car. The girls were busy opening the box of chocolates.

Lilly watched as he motored down the drive. He was heading back to his own unhappy circumstances. For her, it was time to get ready to do the barn chores then put supper on the table, clean up the dishes, help with school work, and fall into bed with a tired, aching body.

Chapter 22

Josiah arrived in Lancaster, Pennsylvania the day after he left from the Boyce station on the Norfolk & Western railroad. The trip meant changing trains a few times, but he wasn't shy about asking questions and found himself on the right trains. He rented a horse for two days from a stable in Lancaster, ten miles from Paradise. A horse would elicit less curiosity than a buggy or wagon and it would be easier to keep out of sight. Besides, renting a horse was cheaper than renting a buggy or wagon.

Josiah knew the road Rebecca would take to the young people's meeting. His plan was to wait along the route, hidden from view, pray she was alone, and that she would go along with his plan. If Rebecca decided to stay, he would have made an attempt to help and he would not feel guilty later.

Josiah rode the horse along the road to Paradise, prepared to sleep in the woods if necessary. The countryside was relatively flat with neat prosperous farms. He knew the families who lived in them. A few gray buggies passed him on the road, driven by men he probably knew. Josiah wore English clothes with the collar of his jacket turned up to shadow his face and block the cool air. He paid no attention to the Amish passengers in the buggies nor did they to him as he rode the horse along the road.

When he found a copse of trees, where he could tether the horse and keep it out of view of the road, he left the hard-packed dirt road and guided the horse into the middle of a grove of fir trees. From a slight rise he had a clear view of the lane Rebecca would take to the main road.

He waited three hours until he saw a buggy coming down the lane. He sprang from his fortification to head her off before she reached the road. She must have spotted him because the horse stopped and the buggy began to turn around.

"Rebecca! It's Josiah!" he shouted to be heard.

The horse stopped again while the buggy was in mid-turn.

Josiah ran as fast as he could and was out of breath when he reached the spot where Rebecca sat holding the reins. "Josiah? Can it really be you?"

He took off his hat so she could see his sandy hair and clear blue eyes. "Have I changed that much in four years?"

She started to cry and hopped off the buggy into his arms. "Oh, Josiah. *Ich* have missed you so."

He patted her back as he did when she was a little girl. "I came to get you. Do you want to leave?"

She had backed away from his arms and dried her tears with her apron. "*Ya*, I am so afraid. Do you remember that man they will insist I marry?"

He did. "I'm sure the reason our parents want you to marry him is because he owns land and a business. I guess their thinking is that you will be well taken care of."

Rebecca was almost as tall as her brother. Her hair was the color of chestnuts, her skin creamy, and her eyes as pretty a brown as his were blue.

"My plan is to take you back to Virginia with me. I work on a farm and the woman who hired me said you can stay at the place until you are able to be on your own."

"How can I get away? The only reason they let me go to the young people's meeting is because it's a prayer meeting and Grace usually comes with me. She wasn't feeling well today."

They sat side by side in the buggy. Josiah didn't want to be seen. "Come with me now. I have a horse across the way. We can ride into Lancaster and catch a train."

She looked at him with wide eyes. "I couldn't do that. *Daed* and *Mamm* would worry." She shook her head and the white cap on her head wiggled from side to side. "No, I just can't leave without them knowing."

"Rebecca, I don't have time to argue. Your horse knows the way to take the buggy back home. Do you have a pencil?"

"In my bag. I use it to underline passages."

"Tear a page out of your bible. You can write that you are going to Virginia with Josiah."

"Josiah! Isn't that sacrilegious?"

He smiled at her. "To go with your brother or tear a page from your bible?"

"You know what I mean," she said.

She sat for a long moment. Josiah kept an eye on the main road. "You are my brother and I trust you do what is best for me. I know I have to leave. There is nothing at home but another set of clothes and my nightgown. "No trappings," as *Daed* has a habit of saying."

Once more, he wanted to be sure. "You have given this much thought?"

She nodded assertively. "*Ya,* I have cried myself to sleep more than one time. In truth, I have wanted to go since you left. I will miss Grace. She's married now, but she still goes to the young people's meetings." Then she laughed. "Grace agrees with me about Abraham. She said she couldn't stand the old buzzard either and couldn't imagine being married to him."

Rebecca sighed deeply. "I am ready once I've written the note to *Mamm* and *Daed* and headed the horse in the direction of home. I can write to Grace once I'm settled."

Rebecca scribbled the note and placed it under the seat cushion. Her father would look there because he insisted the cushion be hung in the barn.

They waited until a buggy went by on the main road. Josiah helped Rebecca down, fixed the reins and tapped the horse in the direction of home. He grabbed Rebecca's hand and they ran across the road to where the rented horse waited. He untethered the horse and gave Rebecca a hand up to sit behind him. It would be fifteen minutes before the horse and buggy arrived at the Blyer house. Josiah knew his father would waste no time in coming after Rebecca. If they were lucky they would reach the station before him and a train to York would be due without a long wait.

Josiah bought the tickets. The train to York would not arrive for another half-hour. He suggested they wait outside the station away from the questioning glances of an English man with a younger Amish woman.

"I saw you signed your name Bly instead of Blyer," said Rebecca.

"Once I left, I started a new life," he replied.

As they sat across the street watching the people coming and going into the railroad station and the busyness on the streets, a buggy he recognized as the one he had sent back to the Blyer house came into view.

"Rebecca, I believe our luck has run out."

She startled and looked in the direction where he pointed. The buggy was a block away, yet there was no mistaking her father and the man sitting next to him. They were both bigger than Josiah.

"Abraham!" she exclaimed. "It's *Daed* and Abraham. Josiah what are we going to do?"

"We will stay over here where we are sheltered from the station."

"Oh, *ya,*" she lamented. "You know they will go in and ask if there has been an Amish girl in there recently."

He smiled. "You're a dead giveaway with that white cap on your head."

"How can you be so calm? *Ich* dare not remove it."

"Rebecca, if you are going to leave the Order, now is the best time to start. Put your cap in your bag."

She did as he asked, so frightened was she that her *Daed* would see them.

They watched from a distance as the two Amish men left the buggy and entered the station. Abraham was a big man with a long beard and a stern face. Josiah remembered the ornery man well.

Josiah pulled a red bandanna from the bag he carried. "Here, tie this around your head." Then he pulled out a brown canvas poncho. "Lay this across your lap so it will cover the blue of your dress showing under your coat." Josiah put his arm around her shoulders and drew her close.

A few minutes later the men come out of the station. They looked around before they split up and searched all about. They looked across where Josiah and Rebecca sat and saw only an English man and his wife sitting on a bench.

Josiah heard a train approaching. It was time for their train to York. "We don't have a choice, Rebecca. We need to be on that train."

She grabbed his hand. "*Ich* don't want to go back."

"Then we will have to confront them. We have to make that train."

They stood up. Rebecca was about to remove the poncho to fold it up when she saw her father and Abraham turn to go back to the buggy. "Wait, Josiah. They're leaving."

He turned from picking up his bag.

The men climbed up to the front seat and sat for a moment before they turned the buggy around to head back to Paradise.

Josiah stuffed the poncho into his bag. He grabbed Rebecca's hand and they ran to the station where they boarded the train to York.

Once in the seat they both sighed with relief. "I feel like a teenager running away from home instead of a grown man rescuing his sister," he said.

"You couldn't have stopped them, they would have pulled me into the buggy."

Josiah knew his sister was right. "Might have," he said.

Chapter 23

Lilly had sewed the sheets and pillowcase for the chaise. She embroidered three roses on the edge of the pillowcase to add color to the bland material. As the clerk had suggested, Lilly put baking soda in the wash water and the muslin softened.

The room off the parlor where Rebecca would stay was cold but Lilly couldn't help that. The best she could do was leave the down quilt for a cover. In a few days it would be March. Spring would have to come sometime.

Three lambs had been born, without complications, in Josiah's absence. Lilly was careful to keep the bedding dry, provide fresh water and feed the mothers well. The lambs looked healthy and she wanted both the ewes and their offspring to stay that way. The tails could be cut off when Josiah returned, which she hoped would be soon. Lilly was tired of feeding, watering, milking the cow, mucking out the barn, and listening to Emily and Flossie's complaints. She didn't blame them. She would complain too, if it would do any good.

Lilly had finished milking the cow and was carrying the pail of milk to the house when she saw two figures coming onto the drive from the main road. She continued to the house and placed the pail on a table on the side porch before she went back outside to meet them.

As they neared, she waved. "Josiah, thank God you are back safe. I was concerned."

"It's good to be back. Mrs. Pierce. This is my sister, Rebecca."

Rebecca gave a shy smile and nod of her head.

Lilly had expected she would be a small, petite young lady. That wasn't the vision of the young woman who stood taller than she. She took Rebecca's hand. "We are so pleased to have you. Come inside, the girls are finishing up their schoolwork."

They went into the kitchen. Emily and Flossie looked up and dropped their pencils on the table before they jumped from their chairs.

"Girls, this is Miss Rebecca, Mr. Bly's sister. Rebecca, I would like to have you meet my daughters, Emily and Flossie"

"Hello, Miss Rebecca," said Emily.

"Momma fixed up your room," said Flossie.

Rebecca offered a sweet smile.

"I'll show you where you will be staying," said Lilly.

Rebecca carried only a handbag. Perhaps she had a trunk on the way.

Josiah answered that unspoken question. "We had to leave in a hurry. There wasn't time for Rebecca to go to the house."

Arriving with only the clothes on her back? How forsaken this young woman must feel.

"At least you are here," said Lilly. "I'll show you the room. You can hang your coat and leave your bag there."

Josiah had waited for Lilly's return. He had been listening to the girls tell him about what went on while he was gone. His smile was warm as he addressed Lilly, "I hear you have three lambs."

"Three I didn't have to help. You can't imagine how delighted I am to know that you will be here for the others that are coming."

"When the lambs were born, Momma said it would be at a time like this that you had to leave."

Lilly felt the color rise in her face. "You don't have to repeat everything I say, Emily."

Josiah chuckled. "I'll take a look at the animals."

With a nod of her head, Lilly agreed. "You and Rebecca must be famished. I'm sure it has been a long trip for you both. I'll prepare supper and we will all have a good meal."

He placed his hand on the door knob to leave before he turned to look at her. "Mrs. Pierce. Thank you."

Rebecca re-braided her long hair and wound the braid at the nape of her neck. She looked unsure of what was expected of her when she entered the kitchen.

Lilly turned from the sink and offered a warm smile. "Do you speak English?"

The young Amish woman came alive. "*Ya!*" She caught herself and giggled. "I am sorry. My English is good but sometimes I slip into the Pennsylvania Dutch."

Lilly laughed aloud. Any tension in the kitchen dissipated.

"I am getting supper ready. If you would like to help you may peel the carrots and cut them up."

Thankful to have something to do, Rebecca picked up a paring knife and went to work.

"Emily when you and Flossie are through, you may set the table."

"Let's use the pretty dishes and eat in the dining room," said Flossie.

"You silly, we don't have time for that. Do we Momma?"

"Emily, it is not nice to call your sister, silly." Lilly looked at them both. "Flossie that was thoughtful and I wish we could. What Emily means is that it takes too much time to prepare for a lovely table setting. I'm sure you remember how long it took at Christmas."

"But you set up the kitchen table nice when Mr. Bly came," said Flossie.

Those words caught Rebecca's attention.

Lilly was quick to respond. "That was because he was a guest. We are all going to sit down as a family."

A light smile creased the new visitor's lips.

When Josiah returned, the table was set and there was a pleasant aroma of baked chicken in the room. Carrots and potatoes had been baked together and Lilly had made a squash casserole. Rebecca made baking powder biscuits.

"I could smell the food out in the changing room. It made me realize how hungry I am. We haven't eaten since we had a bowl of oatmeal at breakfast."

"There is plenty of food," Lilly said. "Rebecca was a big help. I can't wait to bite into one of those biscuits. Go ahead and sit. The girls have put another chair to the table for Rebecca."

Talk was lively between mouthfuls of food. The girls talked about school and Josiah told about the train rides and the countryside. He didn't tell about Rebecca's rescue. That would be a private conversation with Lilly.

When they were eating their dessert of cherry cobbler, Josiah announced that he would be spending the night in the barn because there would be new lambs before morning.

Lilly filled a jug with water and wrapped a couple of cookies for him to take. After he left with the kerosene lantern, it was time to clean up from supper. Emily and Flossie helped clear the table. Rebecca put a kettle of water on the stove to wash the dishes. When the water was hot, she poured it into the basin and made suds with a bar of soap.

"I believe you have done this before," said Lilly.

Rebecca looked at her with a ready smile. "It was my place to take care of the kitchen. I can also help Josiah in the barn."

Rebecca washed the dishes and Lilly stood aside her drying the clean ones with a kitchen towel.

"Your big brother is good to you." It was stated half as a question.

"Oh, *ya*! When he left our Order four years ago, I cried every time I thought of him."

Lilly couldn't help herself. "What was his wife like? Was she pretty?"

Rebecca rested her hands on the side of the basin and looked out the window above the sink. "Plain. Frail. Very set in the Amish way of life. It was *Daed* and *Mamm* who pushed him into it."

"Do you mean your mother and your father?"

Rebecca shook her head and laughed at herself. "See? I let the other language slip in. Yes, my mother and father would have had me married if I hadn't written to Josiah. I didn't wish to be disobedient, but there are times when a woman has to think for herself."

Lilly wondered how many other twenty-year-old women would have been as astute and brave.

"Josiah tells me once you leave you cannot return."

Rebecca dumped the basin of water into the sink. "That is true. I gave much thought to my leaving, and it is unsettling for me to feel adrift. But, Mrs. Pierce, Abraham is sixty-five and a wealthy, mean old man. I saw the way he treated his first wife."

"How wise you are, Rebecca."

She looked squarely at Lilly. "I am still young and strong. There is little I can't do or learn to do. I believe the Lord has led me here."

Lilly put her arm around Rebecca's shoulders. "We are pleased you are here."

"Josiah told me that your husband died last year. I am sorry."

The day she found Frank dead in the barn flashed through her mind. "It has been almost five months. Sometimes it seems he was never here. I felt the Lord guided Josiah here as He did you. I don't know what I would do without your brother's help. Taking care of things myself is a whole new world. My husband took care of everything, except for the housework."

Rebecca chuckled. "The Amish women must learn it all."

Lilly wiped the basin dry. "I have a nightgown that was given to me. I was going to cut it down. You may have it if you like."

Rebecca wiped her hands on her apron. "I would. I only have what clothes were on my back."

"You know what, Rebecca? When we get a good weather day, you and I will ride into Berryville. You can pick out material for a new dress. In the meantime I'll see what material I have in my chest upstairs. There might be enough to fashion a simple house dress."

She could tell from the pleasant smile on Rebecca's wholesome face that idea appealed to her.

Chapter 24

Large pieces of material, enough to make a dress, were not found in Lilly's chest except for a mustard color cotton, which someone had given to her. Who would want a dress of that distasteful color? Lilly had intended to dye the cloth but she never got around to it. She was embarrassed to show it to Rebecca.

"This is all I could find."

Rebecca never skipped a beat. "It will work fine, Mrs. Pierce."

"You may call me Lilly if you like."

A shy look appeared on Rebecca's comely face. "I will call you Miss Lilly, with your permission."

Lilly nodded her approval. "Now we are going to have to make a pattern for a dress."

"No, Miss Lilly, I had to make the one I have on. All I will need are shears, a measuring stick, some pins, a needle and thread."

"We can sew it on the machine."

"Machine?" said a surprised Rebecca.

"I have a sewing machine in the dining room that Mr. Pierce bought for me. I have made most of Emily's and Flossie's clothes."

"I don't know how to work a machine."

Lilly laughed. "You said you could learn to do anything."

Rebecca blushed. "I meant with my hands. I might be afraid of a machine."

"You won't be after I teach you how to use it, and you find how much time it saves." Lilly brought the measuring tape, shears and pins from the sewing machine drawer. "You go ahead and cut out the material and pin it together. When you are ready, we will have lessons on the sewing machine. You will use your hands and your feet."

Rebecca's eyes flew wide open.

They moved the dining room table and chairs and dust mopped so the material could be laid flat on the floor. Lilly watched as Rebecca turned the material exactly where she wanted it, measured, pinned, and began to cut out the dress.

Rebecca threw a questioning look. "This will be shorter than my blue dress. It will come above the tops of my shoes."

"That will be in style. Skirts are worn half-way between ankles and knees. I don't think you will wear this one in public."

Rebecca smiled at Lilly. "I have seen the way the English girls dress. The Amish dress plain."

Lilly sat in a chair and watched the young girl work. "Life is going to be very different for you. Do you want to dress the way the English girls dress?"

Rebecca sat back on her knees. "I have thought about it. I wish I was small like most of them."

"Rebecca you are an attractive young woman. I don't think there is a woman alive who wouldn't change something about her person. When we go into Berryville, we will find the right patterns for you. My niece's friend, Lottie, used to work as a seamstress. I'm sure she would be glad to help us."

While Rebecca pinned the pieces of cloth together, Lilly removed the wooden cover to the White treadle sewing machine. She found the closest matching thread to the dress material and wound it on a bobbin. Then she threaded the needle. She had practice material once it was time to give Rebecca her first lesson.

It was almost time for Emily and Flossie to return from school. They never dawdled because they were overjoyed to have Rebecca there. So was Lilly. Rebecca was good company and a great help in cleaning, getting meals and entertaining the girls. More than once Rebecca went to the barn to help Josiah. She was the one who held the lambs when he cut off their tails, and she was the one who lent a hand with ewes in trouble with delivering lambs. Lilly thought Rebecca was more help than an extra hired man.

Even Ef seemed pleased to have another person around, especially one who would pet her and throw her a scrap of food.

Lilly wanted to get the sewing lesson over before the girls returned from school.

Chapter 25

Rebecca was pleased to have two dresses to wear. The mustard-colored dress went well with her chestnut hair and creamy complexion. It did come above her tall shoes, which she said was fine. It was easier for her to move around.

Lilly phoned Addie. She wanted to know if Lottie would help them find patterns and material for Rebecca.

Addie said Lottie was getting close to the time for the new baby to arrive, but she would ask her.

Addie phoned back, "Aunt Lilly, Lottie said she would love to get out of the house. She will have to bring Little Cal with her. I'll drive them in the buggy. We can meet you at Coyner's store at nine o'clock on Thursday."

"That would be perfect, Addie. Do you think we would have time to visit your mother?"

"I don't see why not. I'll get word to her. She can ask Mrs. Foster to come over, too."

"I'm sure Lottie's mother would like that. Addie, you are a dear. I can't wait for you to meet Rebecca. We will see you on Thursday."

"Aunt Lilly, you sound happy."

"I am. It is the first time in six months that I have felt like myself."

She heard Addie chuckle. "I can hardly wait for Thursday. Good-bye."

"Good-bye Addie."

**

Emily and Flossie were disappointed they couldn't make the trip into Berryville. Lilly said school was more important.

Josiah would take Ef to the barn with him, and he would see the girls were all right if they arrived home before the travelers.

There was a March breeze. Rebecca wore her blue dress and black wool coat. Lilly gave her a black knitted hat to keep her head warm. They took quilts to lay over their laps. Jack was harnessed and ready for the six-mile trip. The women climbed into the front seat with Lilly holding the reins.

Rebecca was nervous. "What will these ladies think of me?"

"They will think you are the lovely person you are. Addie and Lottie are not many years older than you."

"It makes my stomach jumpy to meet new people. Miss Lilly, I know this will cost money. How can I repay you?"

"You have already repaid me with your help. This is going to be an enjoyable day for all of us. Put on that pretty smile."

Rebecca looked over at her with a wide grin. "Miss Lilly, you make me feel *gut.*"

Lilly turned and laughed. "*Ya,* I think that means good."

"You are learning," said the former Amish young woman who, at times, slipped into Pennsylvania Dutch.

They reached Berryville where Lilly pointed out the Hawthorne House, Irene Butler's dress shop, the Bank of Clarke County, the general store and the hotel. She spotted Addie's buggy parked across the street from the department store. Lottie sat beside her.

Lilly parked next to the buggy and pulled Jack to a stop. She called to them as she left her seat and secured the reins to a post. "Good morning."

"Good morning, Aunt Lilly. Lottie and I got an early start." Addie hopped out of the buggy, tied the reins, and came to help Lottie down.

"Hello, Mrs. Pierce," said Lottie. "I'm not as sure-footed as I was." The short Lottie was round as a barrel.

Rebecca came around the buggy to stand next to Lilly.

"Adelaide Lockwood and Lottie Dunn meet Rebecca Blyer."

Addie took Rebecca's hand. "Aunt Lilly tells me you are Josiah Bly's sister."

"I am. Josiah shortened his name. I may also do the same."

Lottie offered a big smile. "I don't think it matters. It's nice to meet you, Rebecca."

"Where is your little boy, Lottie? Addie said you would bring him," said Lilly.

"Caleb took him to follow him around for the day. He said I needed some time without having to worry about keeping an eye on a two-year-old."

"Not many men are that understanding," said Lilly.

"Well, let's not stand here in the street any longer," said Adelaide.

"Yes, time to go in and see Nosy Nettie."

"Lottie Bell, you shouldn't say things like that," chided Addie. "Maybe she doesn't work here anymore."

"She'll work here until she's sixty," said Lottie. "Where else can she keep up on the news?"

Rebecca looked puzzled.

"Addie and Lottie are like sisters and have been friends since elementary school," said Lilly as a way of explaining their casual patter. "They took an adventurous trip to Colorado three years ago."

"My goodness," exclaimed Rebecca. "I would never be that brave."

"Aunt Lilly said you left your Amish way of life. That takes more courage than I have," said Addie.

"It was a choice between leaving and marrying a mean, sixty-five-year-old man."

"I wouldn't call that any choice at all," said Lottie. "You are young."

"I will be twenty-one in May."

"Addie you were concerned because Alex is sixteen years older than you. What if he was forty-five years older?" said Lottie.

"I don't even want to think about it," answered Addie. "Watch your step. You probably can't see over your tummy."

"Guide me up. I may have to go through the door sideways."

All four ladies laughed.

Lottie and Rebecca looked over the patterns while Lilly and Addie wandered around the store marveling at what new items had been added.

"Rebecca, let's find skirt, waist and dress patterns. The patterns will be the same but with a variety of materials they will look different. None of us are built alike. We'll find designs that will look good for your frame. How tall are you?"

With a pink blush to her cheeks and quiet voice, she replied, "I am five-feet and nine inches."

Lottie looked up at her. "You are lucky to be tall."

"I wish I was slim."

Lottie smiled at her. "You are the right size."

"Miss Lottie, all of the Amish women dress the same."

"You said you weren't going to be Amish anymore."

"True," agreed Rebecca.

Nettie was still clerking. She was waiting on another customer, which Lottie was pleased about. When she finished that transaction, Nettie came to where Lottie was looking at patterns.

"Lottie Bell. You are expecting another baby?"

Lottie looked at her with an, isn't it obvious look.

Nettie eyed Rebecca from her head to her toes. "Is this your friend?"

"Yes, she is." Lottie went back to the pattern search without introducing them.

"Are you visiting?" Nettie asked Rebecca.

Rebecca started to speak but Lottie cut her off. "She is visiting Mrs. Pierce. We came for patterns and material."

Nettie shrugged a shoulder. "You are here at a good time. We recently received a shipment and the choices are endless." Nettie was off to display the myriad bolts of fabric.

When they were through, there was enough material for two skirts, two blouses and two dresses. The cotton material was both heavy weight and light weight in stripes, checks and plain colors.

Lilly was in a buying mood. She bought Rebecca a pair of knee socks, lisle stockings, and a set of underpinnings. Rebecca couldn't be happier when Lilly showed her what she was buying.

Lilly bought chocolates for Emily and Flossie and a pair of work gloves for Josiah. Then she spied two lace doilies and bought one each to give to Laura and Lottie's mother. It felt like Christmas. The bill came to thirty-four dollars and twenty-five cents. It was more than Lilly wanted to pay, but today was a special day. Perhaps she could sell a few lambs to make up for it.

Nettie was kept so busy cutting material and preparing the bill she didn't have time to pry. She zipped thirty-five dollars up on the cable to Mr. Coyner's spot on the landing and he zipped back the change.

"Come in again when we can find time to chat," Nettie called as the foursome headed toward the door.

Outside the door Lottie said under her breath, "How about in five years."

Addie couldn't help smiling. "Lottie, behave yourself."

Chapter 26

Lottie's mother was at Laura's house when the two buggies arrived. The women came to the door and onto the porch as the visitors stepped to the ground: Lottie, well into pregnancy, Addie, Lilly, and Rebecca, who towered over the other three.

Rebecca took the reins to hitch Jack to a post. Lilly hurried to the porch and hugged Laura and greeted Mrs. Foster. Addie was holding Lottie's arm as they mounted the two steps.

Lottie's mother hugged her daughter tightly. "Lottie, you shouldn't have left the house. You need to be careful so near your term. Are you all right?"

"I was happy to get away. It has been a long winter. I'm a little edgy and lopsided but, otherwise, I feel great."

Rebecca came onto the porch. Lilly introduced her and the six women went into the house to have lunch and catch up on news.

"Lottie's mother brought her linen tablecloth, silver and china," explained Laura, not wanting her sister to think it was hers. She didn't have to explain, Lilly knew Laura wasn't into the finer things in life.

"I have little use for it," said Lottie's mother, whose husband was another hired man on the farm with a penchant for alcohol. "We used to entertain his customers before we moved here."

The unexplained words were that her husband lost his business because of the drinking and took a few steps down working on the farm. Lilly, Lottie and Addie all knew the story.

Rebecca was taking in the one room that served as kitchen and living room. "Your house is very comfortable, Mrs. Richards."

Laura's smile was wide. No one had ever told her she had a comfortable house. "Thank you."

Mrs. Foster was getting plates of food ready.

"Everyone hang up your wraps and take a seat," said Laura.

"Can we help?" asked Addie.

"No. This is our treat. Once we put the food on the table and pour the tea, we will be ready to hear what is going on in your lives," said Lottie's mother.

They served delicate sandwiches, potato soup, a platter of cheese and pickles, and an upside down pineapple cake, a favorite recipe of Lottie's mother. The women talked for two hours about how the farms were doing, the new baby coming, Charlie and Ella, Clay's problem with old Mr. Lockwood, the fabric and patterns they had bought, and what it was like to be Amish.

It was close to two o'clock when lunch was over and they were ready to leave. Lilly could tell that Laura had taken a liking to Rebecca. She even gave her a hug good-bye. It was highly unusual for Laura to let her feelings show.

Lilly drove the buggy up the main street of Berryville before she turned onto the Berryville-White Post road. "I told you we were going to have an enjoyable day. How do you feel, Rebecca?"

"I feel the English women are not so different from the Amish."

"What do you think of the patterns and material Lottie picked out for you?"

"I have not worn light colors except for blue. Miss Lottie told me what material should be used for skirts, blouses and dresses. She said I would have to add about five or six inches to the length of the pattern. I think she knows much about sewing." Rebecca hesitated. "Miss Lilly, if her mother can't help her when the baby comes, I could go."

"What a very nice offer," replied Lilly, although she didn't care for the thought of Rebecca not being at the house.

The girls came running from the big farmhouse when the buggy came up the lane, and Josiah came out of the barn with Ef at his heels.

"Momma, we're glad you're back. I was worried," said Flossie, always the concerned one.

"Did you get pretty material?" asked Emily.

"Very pretty," answered Rebecca.

"And, I brought a present for you girls and one for Mr. Bly," Lilly informed.

"Did you bring one for Ef?" asked Flossie.

Lilly laughed. "I didn't see any dog presents."

Josiah came up as they alighted the conveyance.

"Mrs. Pierce, I'll take care of Jack and the buggy."

"Thank you, Josiah." Lilly was in a good mood. "You may call me Miss Lilly, if you would like."

Josiah's blue eyes were gentle. "I would like that," he said.

"You girls help us carry these packages into the house." Lilly turned to Rebecca. "We will have to make a simple supper. We're later than I thought we would be."

"*Ya!* Such a *gut* time we had."

Lilly put her arm around Rebecca's shoulders. "*Ya!*"

Chapter 27

Clayton Lockwood had written to his former army pal, Slick. His given name was Anthony Vello. People called him Tony. He had written back that he wasn't married, and getting out of New York City sounded good to him. He would like to come and help his army buddy out. He didn't know how long he could stay.

Clay was relieved. Frances Gray was getting antsy to leave as she had another position offered. Tony's arrival would allow Clay time to keep looking.

Anthony Vello arrived on the six-forty train. Clay drove his father's Model-T Ford up to the Bluemont train station to get him. It wasn't difficult to pick him out among the passengers. A dapper man, he wore a bowler hat, an expensive tan camelhair overcoat and carried a leather suitcase. He hadn't changed much: average build, black hair, smooth shaven, olive complexion. Anthony Vello carried himself erect. He wasn't handsome, but there was something about him that made people take a second look. When he got into the car, Clay noticed a diamond ring on Tony's little finger. It appeared Anthony Vello was doing well. Clay reached over and shook his hand.

"You don't know how glad I am to see you," said Clay.

His former army friend flashed a pearly-white smile. "You don't know how glad I am to be here," answered Tony. "Your letter came at the right time. I was thinking of taking a vacation. Why not in Virginia and give you a hand?"

Clay pulled the choke and turned the key. He pulled the shift lever on the wheel into drive, lifted his foot from the clutch and they were on their way. "We'll take it slow because these headlamps don't pick up too far ahead. The road is curvy as we wind down the mountain. How has life been treating you since you got out?"

"I can't complain," said Tony. "Tell me about your father. I thought you wanted to go back and finish at the university and open a drug store."

"Plans change," said Clay. "I am trying to run a farm. My father is in his own world."

Tony chuckled. "I took care of a lot of them in the service. They were younger and couldn't handle the war. It might be nice to escape from the real world once in a while."

"Yeah," agreed Clay. "But the real world would be right there when you return."

"People try to escape. Lots of dope-heads in New York City. You can buy that stuff right over the counter and get hooked on it." Tony laughed. "You oughta' open a drug store. You could make a bundle."

"I wouldn't want to make it that way," said Clay.

They reached the house. Clay lifted Tony's suitcase. "The maid's name is Faith. She's a great

cook so you'll have good food while you're here."
Clay opened the door to the kitchen. "I'll show you
to your room and you can freshen up. Those train
rides are tiring."

"Nice place you've got here," Tony observed
as he followed Clay.

"It takes a lot to keep it going. I'll show you
around the place tomorrow. We moved Father's
room here on the first floor. We were afraid he
would fall down the stairs. Ideas pop into his head
and he starts to wander. He's fallen a few times. Do
you want to go in to see him?"

"Might as well."

Clay opened a door and placed Tony's
suitcase inside. "You'll be staying here. It connects
with Father's room. Mrs. Gray, the lady who cared
for him, left this morning."

Clay opened the door to this father's room
and was surprised to see Faith sitting in a chair. She
rose when they entered.

"Chip had to leave so I came to sit with the
Mister until you got back," she explained.

"Thank you, Faith. This is Mr. Vello. He
will be helping me with father for a while."

Anthony Vello gave a big smile to the black
lady before him. "If I call you, Faith, you are to call
me Tony."

Faith was not shy about sizing up Clay's
friend. Clay wasn't sure she approved

She was firm. "No, sir. That wouldn't be
right. I will call you Mister Tony."

He chuckled. "I kind of like that, Miss Faith."

She shook her head. "I'll be puttin' your meal on the table. Your daddy is sleepin' hard."

Clay and Tony ate a supper of baked ham, sweet potatoes, turnips, and cornbread with peach cobbler for dessert."

"I'll have to be careful I don't pile on some pounds while I'm here," remarked Tony. "I haven't had a feast like this for a long time."

When the cook brought more coffee, he said, "I may have to take you back to New York City with me, Miss Faith."

"I know my place," she remarked.

After dinner and conversation, Tony went to his room. He looked in on Clay's father, sound asleep. Tony hoped he would stay that way through the night. He was weary, physically and emotionally. This arrangement was going to work out fine. He unpacked his suitcase and placed his 45 caliber pistol in the top drawer of the bureau. He wouldn't be needing that for a while.

Chapter 28

Lilly picked up the phone. Who would be calling at five o'clock in the morning?

"Aunt Lilly, I hope I didn't wake you."

"Addie! For heaven's sake what is wrong?"

"I just got home from delivering Lottie's baby."

Lilly's heart skipped a beat. "Has something happened to Lottie...or the baby?"

"No. I'm in a euphoric state. I remembered everything from helping deliver Sarah Jane. He's a beautiful baby."

"Why are you calling so early? Rebecca and I have just started getting breakfast ready."

"I have a favor to ask. Lottie's mother is sick and she can't come to help. Do you think Rebecca could come for a few days? Just until Mrs. Foster gets over her cold."

"How do you know Mrs. Foster is ill?"

"Charlie told me yesterday when he came up to see Ella. He said Lottie's mother worried that the baby would come and Lottie wouldn't have anyone to help her with Little Cal. I have to take care of the office because Alex is spending most of his time helping Caleb. The spring calves have started to arrive."

"Addie, I've never heard you sound so rattled. Hold on. I'll pose the question to Rebecca."

Rebecca was more than willing.

"She will come, Addie. When do you want me to bring her up?"

"I wish I could send Alex with the Franklin, but I know he can't spare the time."

"I don't mind bringing her. We'll finish up breakfast and get the girls off to school. We can't get there until around ten."

"Oh, thank you. I sent Ella down to stay with Lottie. I'm sorry if I caused any alarm. I didn't know what else to do."

"You did the right thing," assured Lilly. "Good-bye, Addie."

"Bye, Aunt Lilly. I can't thank you enough."

Lilly hung up the receiver and turned to Rebecca. "Isn't this a fine kettle of fish."

The young woman looked puzzled.

"Never mind. We'll drop the girls at school and go on up to *Lockwood*. Rebecca, run out to the barn and ask Josiah to hook Jack to the buggy. We have one long day ahead of us."

Emily and Flossie heard the whole conversation.

"I don't see why we can't go to Addie's and see Miss Lottie's new baby," complained Emily. "We never get to do the fun stuff."

"For one thing, you have school. For another, Miss Lottie is very tired. You can see the baby some other time."

"I wish Rebecca didn't have to go," said Flossie. "She will come back, won't she?"

164

When it was time to go, Rebecca came to the buggy carrying a satchel Lilly had loaned to her. "What sad faces," she remarked. "Sure, I'll be back, my little friends. Don't you think it is important to help Miss Lottie?"

The girls shook their heads in agreement. They still wanted to go.

It was an eleven mile trip to *Lockwood*. Rebecca was in awe of the large, white stucco house with big columns that sat majestically on the hill.

"That is where Alex and Addie live," Lilly pointed out. "We'll stop there before we go to Lottie's."

Addie saw them coming up the long lane leading to the house and came out the back door. She had a heavy shawl over her shoulders. She waved to them and climbed into the back seat when the buggy stopped.

"This has been an interesting morning," she greeted them. "I have been up since three o'clock. That's when Caleb came running up to the house to tell me Lottie's water had broken and she was in pain."

"You're still excited," remarked Lilly. "I thought you wanted to be far away when this happened."

"I did. But everything went so fast, I had no choice. Good morning, Rebecca."

"Good morning, Miss Addie."

They drove down the farm lane to the brick house where Caleb and Lottie lived. Lilly tied Jack to a post. Rebecca pulled the satchel from the floor of the buggy and the three went inside.

165

Ella was in the kitchen making breakfast. The worried look drained from her face when they entered. "Miss Addie, I'm glad you're back!" The young lady was a good cook and housekeeper, but she was leery of acting as a caretaker.

"This is Rebecca," Addie said. "She has come to take over."

Lottie called from her bedroom. "I hear you out there and I smell food."

"Ella, you can go back to the house. Hold on, Lottie, I'm coming." Addie motioned for Lilly and Rebecca to follow her in.

"How are you doing?" asked Adelaide.

"I'm sore, tired and hungry," answered Lottie. "Hello, Mrs. Pierce and Rebecca."

Lilly moved to the bedside and kissed Lottie on the cheek. "I hear you have a beautiful baby boy."

Lottie smiled. "I don't think I've been awake enough to realize that. He's bundled up in his cradle. It won't be long before he's hungry and lets us know he is on the earth."

"Ella made breakfast, Lottie. Do you feel like eating?" asked Addie.

"I'm starved."

Rebecca spoke. "Miss Lottie, I will stay with you until your mother comes. I'll fix you a tray of food."

"Thank you, Rebecca. There is a room upstairs that I had ready for my mother. You may use that while you're here. Do you know about new mothers and babies?"

"I have taken care of many," she replied before she went to the kitchen.

Lilly went to the cradle. The baby was a good size with coal black hair. His little face was red and he was sound asleep. As she looked down on him a lump came to her throat as she thought of her dear little CJ. She said a silent prayer that this little one would be healthy.

Lilly turned from the cradle. "Have you given him a name?"

"Caleb wants to name him Jess."

"After his friend that married the Irish girl?"

"Yes."

"Where did they go?" asked Lilly.

Lottie shrugged a shoulder and let out a sigh. "Jess said he wanted to try his luck in California and Fannie said she was all for it. That was last September. We haven't heard whether they made it or not."

"Alex misses having Jess on the farm. I wish they would both come back," lamented Addie.

Rebecca brought in the tray with eggs, bacon, toast and milk. She helped Lottie get situated with pillows at her back and placed the tray over her lap.

Little Cal woke up. Addie went upstairs to get him from his crib. She dressed him and carried him down to his mother's room.

Lottie had finished most of the breakfast and pushed the tray aside so she could hold Cal. She smoothed his hair back and kissed him. "Good morning, sweet boy. You are going to have a friend to play with as you both grow."

Cal looked at his mother and scampered off the bed.

Rebecca seemed right at home. She took the toddler to the kitchen to feed him.

When they left, Lilly told Addie to call her as soon as Mrs. Foster was available. She would come for Rebecca. Addie said she would.

It was a lonely eleven miles back to Boyce. Lilly had grown fond of the tall, Amish young woman in the one month she had come to live with them. The house would be lonesome without her.

Josiah came to get Jack and the buggy when Lilly drove up.

"Did all go well?"

"Yes, it was a good trip. Rebecca is comfortable. I told Addie I would come back to get her when Lottie's mother was able to help."

Josiah leaned on the rim of the buggy. "It is good for Rebecca to be out and seeing what her new life will be like. She will be needing to be out on her own."

"Perhaps I can pay her as an extra hired hand. She is a great help."

"Miss Lilly, I understand what you are saying. For Rebecca, I think it will be better if she lives out among others."

Lilly considered what he said. "You are probably right. The girls and I enjoy her company."

"As do I," he agreed. "What is best for us may not be best for her."

Josiah hopped into the buggy and went to the barn. Lilly went into the house. There was laundry waiting.

Chapter 29

Tony Vello had been taking care of Mr. Lockwood for two weeks. Clay had no complaints. At times, Clay helped when more than two hands were required. Other times, when his father was asleep, he and Tony played cards and talked about their time in the service. Tony had not been forthcoming about his life after the war. Clay decided to ask him point blank what he did to appear so prosperous. They were sitting at the dining room table smoking cigars.

Tony decided to share his story. "You know I didn't have the kind of schooling you had. There wasn't much for me to look forward to after the war. I was twenty-eight when the war ended and came home without having gained any occupation, except as an orderly. I didn't want to work at that for the rest of my life. I knew a guy in the numbers racket before I went in the army so I looked him up."

Clay flicked the ashes from his cigar and leaned back in his chair listening intently.

Tony continued. "He was a decent guy and was making lots of money. He let me work for him. When I got enough money together, I bought a piece of a boxer. The fight game is big business. The first boxer I put my money into did well. He was never going to be big-time, but he was honest and won enough fights to sweeten the pot."

"And knowing you, you couldn't put the money in the bank, you put it into another boxer," said Clay.

A wry smile appeared. "Yeah, I couldn't resist. This kid showed a lot of promise. He'd won more than he'd lost and I liked his style. Four people put money in to back him. I didn't know the other three. That's where I went wrong. They picked the fights he was to win and the ones he was supposed to throw. I had a lot of money riding on him winning the last bout. At the last minute I found out he wasn't supposed to win. I couldn't afford to lose that money, so I convinced him that he was a better boxer and should let people see how good he was."

"Let me guess," said Clay. "He won, but your partners had put money on the other boxer and you are in the dog house. That's why my letter was in time and why you decided to come down here."

"Just until the heat is off. Maybe it wasn't fair to you. They play rough, Clay. I had to get out of town."

"It doesn't make any difference to me as long as they don't find out you're here. I was in a bind and you came to help. It's probably best for you to take time to sort things out. You might like farming."

Tony howled. "The closest I want to get to a horse is watching a race."

Clay turned serious. "You are welcome to stay as long as necessary."

"Thanks. Are you still searching for a replacement for me?"

Clay nodded. "Still looking. Not having any luck."

That night Clay thought about his friend and had a touch of empathy for him. Tony hadn't left the house since he arrived. Clay decided to take him up to *Lockwood* to show him what a thriving cattle farm looks like.

**

The next morning, Chip came to spend the time with Mr. Lockwood while Clay and Tony went to see Alex. Getting away for a few hours would be good for them both.

Clay took the Model T, even though he had to raise his voice to be heard over the noisy engine and rattle of the auto. He would have preferred to ride his horse. Tony was not a rider.

"We'll be back around three this afternoon," Clay told Chip.

The teenager liked the extra money he earned watching the old man. It beat mucking out the barn.

The March day was windy and overcast. Tony was well-dressed for a trip to a farm but they were the only type of clothes he owned. Clay's work shirt and pants were sizes too big for Tony. He did wear one of Clay's caps instead of the bowler hat.

When Clay arrived at the farm he decided to drive to the barn rather than go to the house. He was sure Addie would be working in the office.

Tony let out a low whistle. "This is some place."

It was a surprise to see Lilly Pierce's buggy coming from the direction of the brick house where Lottie lived. Lottie, Addie and Clay had spent good times together before Addie got that foolish idea of going to Colorado. He stopped the car and got out.

Lilly drove to where he stood. She pulled back on the reins and halted Jack.

"Mrs. Pierce," Clay greeted her. "I certainly didn't expect to see you here."

"Hello, Clayton. I am as surprised to see you. Do you remember Josiah Bly?"

Clay nodded.

"This is his sister, Rebecca. Rebecca this is Clayton Lockwood, a brother to Alex."

Clay touched his cap acknowledging Rebecca.

She offered a shy smile.

"Rebecca has been helping Lottie for a few days with the new baby."

Clay's eyebrows raised. "Lottie has a new baby? How are they doing?"

"He's a lovely, cuddly baby boy and Lottie is doing well."

Tony had left the automobile and came to stand by Clay.

"This is my friend from the service, Anthony Vello. He is visiting and taking care of Father until I can find someone permanently. Tony, this is Mrs. Lilly Pierce."

Tony came around to the side of the buggy and took Lilly's gloved hand. He flashed a dazzling smile. "It is my pleasure, Mrs. Pierce." He removed his cap and nodded while still holding Lilly's hand. "And, Miss Rebecca."

Rebecca blushed. Lilly felt flustered. Who was this man who talked with some kind of an accent and wore a camelhair coat, silk scarf, leather gloves, and polished shoes to the barn?

"Tony is from New York City. Perhaps you remember me mentioning my three pals in the army."

Lilly remembered: Slick, Bruiser and Squirrel. There was no mistaking that the man who held her hand was the one they called Slick.

"It's nice to meet you, Mr. Vello."

"The name is, Tony," he said. "The pleasure is all mine." He dashed her with his smile once again before he went to stand with Clay.

"How are the girls doing?" Clay inquired.

"Now that Josiah is working for me, all is going well. And, Ef is growing each day. I think she has adopted Josiah. He is training her to be a good farm dog."

"Do you own a farm, Mrs. Pierce?" asked Tony.

"I do. Sheep and a few horses. Alex wants me to start raising the type of cattle he has here. I'm not so sure. I think I will have to get Josiah's opinion about that. Clayton you will have to come for a visit. The girls are always happy to see you."

"Thank you, Mrs. Pierce. I don't get too far away from the house with Father being in the state he is. If you hear of anyone you think would be suitable to care for him, I would breathe a sigh of relief. Tony used to work as an orderly when we were in the army."

Lilly smiled at Tony. "How fortunate you came to help Clayton."

"I couldn't let an army buddy down," he said.

Clay stepped back from the buggy. "I'll let you be on your way. It was good to see you again."

Lilly tapped the reins and Jack started. She sat in quiet contemplation. Who was this friend of Clay's? He was different and she was confused about the warm sensation she felt when he held her hand.

Clay and Tony got back into the car. "I wouldn't take Lilly Pierce for a farmer's wife," said Tony.

"Her husband died six months ago. He was one of those who ruled the roost and never let her get involved with any of the workings of a farm. She has two young girls. It hasn't been easy for any of them. Rumor is that she was left in debt."

Tony replied, "Debt would be the least of my problems."

Clay started the car. "Couldn't you pay them off? Do you think you're going to be able to safely go back to the city?"

Tony didn't answer him. His thoughts were elsewhere. "Your Lilly Pierce is too attractive to have to worry about money."

Clay glanced over at him with a puzzled look. What was on Tony's mind?

Chapter 30

"I am happy to be back," Rebecca said to Lilly as they arrived back at *Roseville*.

Josiah was working next to the barn. He went to greet them. Lilly knew he would park the buggy and take care of Jack.

Rebecca hopped down, ran into his arms and hugged her big brother.

"I'm proud of you," he said. "You were on your own. How did it go?"

"I am learning much about the English ways. Miss Lottie was good to me. She has a toddler and the new baby and…"

"Rebecca," Lilly interrupted. "It's almost lunch time. Josiah, once you put Jack away come into the house for a warm meal and we can hear all about Rebecca's experience, although Lilly had already heard all about it on the way home.

Rebecca was excited. Her eyes widened, "*Ya!*"

They had vegetable soup and ham sandwiches while Rebecca told Josiah about her four days spent at Lottie's. She giggled like a school girl when she finished. "I am glad to be back." Rebecca left the table and went to the room off the parlor she was using.

Lilly poured freshly brewed coffee into mugs before taking her seat at the table. "I looked over Alex's cattle while I was there," she said. "Josiah, I'd like to have you go up and see if you think I should have them here on the farm."

He sipped his coffee and thought about Lilly's statement. "Alex has talked with me about them. I'm not sure I am the one to guide you in that direction."

Lilly put her cup down. "Who else would be? You are the one who takes care of the animals."

He looked directly at her, his blue eyes serious. "I take care of animals I am familiar with."

She felt her ire rise. "Alex says they are hefty meat cattle and he's earning good money on them. I have to have something on this place that is going to pay so I can keep it going!" Why was she being indignant with this man who was the answer to her prayers?

Josiah sat in silence.

"I'm sorry," she said. "There are times when my feelings rule my tongue."

"There is nothing to be sorry for. You have much to think about."

"Don't be so understanding," she said and drank from her cup.

He laughed.

She relaxed, "Josiah, I want to find out about what Alex has in mind. I would like to have you with me when I do."

"Miss Lilly, I will be more than happy to lend whatever assistance I can."

Lilly reached over and touched his sleeve. "Thank you. I depend on you. The best move I have made since Frank died was to lure you away from the Caldwells."

"You were fishing?" he asked with a sly smile. "You caught me hook, line, and sinker."

Lilly's face turned beet red. She pulled her hand back. "I'm not sure I used the right word."

He smiled that catchy smile that said there was more to Josiah Bly than what showed on the surface. "Any time you care to go, I'll be ready. I need to get back to work. Miss Lilly, I have enjoyed our lunch."

Lilly sat in her chair after he left. Her thoughts were about what had just taken place. What had possessed her to put her hand on his sleeve? Had she made a mistake?

Rebecca hurried into the kitchen. "Miss Lilly! You sewed my blouse together."

Lilly's attention turned to the elated young woman. "I had some extra time while you were away. The pieces were all cut and pinned. Try it on and I'll make adjustments if they are needed."

"You are too *gut* to me. I mean good."

Lilly smiled. "We are both tripping over our words today."

Chapter 31

When May came, Lilly had a marketable flock of sheep and lambs. It was time to shear the wool.

Also, the last of the foals was born and all four would bring in some money. Lilly's funds were dwindling.

Josiah suggested she tell Clayton Lockwood that the foal he was interested in had arrived. Lilly called Clayton on the phone. He said he and Tony would come.

Lilly was surprised to hear that man from New York City was still at Clay's place. They were coming the same day as the team of shearers was due. Lilly had to feed the shearers. She might as well feed Clayton and his friend at the same time. Rebecca had helped with feeding a large group many times. Together they planned and prepared.

When shearing day arrived, Lilly allowed Emily and Flossie to stay home from school. Extra hands to help with the serving meant Lilly wouldn't have to pay hired help.

"Don't the other farmers and their wives come to help? The Amish help each other," said Rebecca.

"Another of the English ways you are learning. I pay the shearers and feed them. Haying season is different. Neighbors help each other

180

because all of the farmers need help getting in their hay. Not all farmers raise sheep."

The day was pleasant. That was a boon. Otherwise, shearing inside the barn and feeding men in the house was a messy business.

Clayton and Tony arrived before noon. They went directly to the barn. Lilly caught a glimpse of them from the kitchen window. Tony was dressed in a work shirt and work pants. He wore a cap. Although he was dressed for the barn, he still had that confident bearing that set him apart from other men she knew. He and Clayton were in deep conversation.

Rebecca had shortened the blue Amish dress. She wore it with a flowered bib apron of Lilly's. The ugly mustard-colored dress was set aside to wear in the house on days they did the wash. She and Lilly had fashioned one dress from the material they bought at Coyner's. It was a lovely shade of tan with lace cuffs and collar and pearl buttons down the front. Rebecca wore it to church. She was beginning to like going to the Boyce United Methodist Church on Sundays with Lilly and the girls. Going to church was different from the Amish who went to meetings every other Sunday at another member's house. Rebecca did her best to convince Josiah to go. He said he was happy to hitch Jack to the buggy and send them off.

Lilly prepared the ham and meatloaf while Rebecca sliced loaves of bread and sliced cheese from the wheel of cheese on the back porch. Rebecca made oven fried chicken, noodles and cabbage, and schnitzel beans. Lilly made a potato salad. There were pies and cakes for dessert.

Josiah brought the men up to the house where they were to eat on a long table of boards placed across sawhorses covered with muslin cloth. Lilly wasn't going to use her good linen tablecloths on wool shearers or take a chance on snagging them on splinters.

Clayton and Tony came with them. They took their seats on the benches.

The men were hungry. Lilly, Rebecca, Emily and Flossie hustled between the kitchen and outdoors to get the food on the table. The men didn't wait. As soon as a dish was brought out they dove right in.

Emily and Flossie poured cold tea and water. Lilly and Rebecca handled the coffee and hot tea.

Two long days of preparation and the food was devoured in twenty minutes. The shearers said thank you, wiped their hands on their pants and went back to finish shearing the sheep. Josiah, Clayton, and Tony remained at the table. Josiah and Clay talked about farming while Tony listened with one ear and kept an eye on Lilly.

The women and girls sat down. It was time for them to eat what was left. The girls ate quickly and went off to play. Rebecca finished and began to clear the table.

"Miss Lilly," said Josiah. "You are going to have quite a few bags of wool. I'm culling the lambs and older ewes that will be ready for market. Perhaps that will help offset the cost of a new plow."

"New plow! What's the matter with the one we have?"

"I've tried to salvage it, but it is beyond repair. We still have crops to put in. The sooner you can get a plow the better, if you want to have feed for next winter. Claude is a good plowhorse."

Lilly rested her forehead in her hand before she looked up. "When things are beginning to go well, something pops up to tear it down."

"I'm interested in buying that foal of yours, Mrs. Pierce," said Clayton, hoping to soothe some of Lilly's torment.

Tony rose from his seat and went to sit by Lilly. "In the short time I've been here, I've come to believe that farming is a risky business. I'm of a mind to buy a farm implement store. I could give you a good price on a plow." He winked at her.

Lilly couldn't help but laugh. When she looked over at him, he dazzled her with his smile once again. Although he wore a work shirt, Tony Vello would never be mistaken for a hard-working farmer or even a gentleman farmer. His hands, with a diamond ring on one little finger, were smooth. His olive skin showed no lengthy exposure to the sun, and his carriage was that of a man who was used to an easier way of life.

"Mr. Vello, I believe you could. I thought you were going back to the city life."

""Miss Lilly, you are supposed to call me Tony. Don't you want to make me feel comfortable while I'm here? I've heard that's the southern way."

Josiah cleared his throat. "I'll be heading back to see how it's going. Good-bye Clay." He nodded in Tony's direction.

Lilly turned to Clay. "How is your father doing?"

"Dr. Hawthorne says his heart is weaker. He's confined to bed most of the time. Tony is thinking of returning to New York next week."

"I'm sorry to hear that," Lilly replied. "You won't be able to care for your father without help."

"I've been giving it thought. I know Josiah's sister helped Lottie. I wondered if she would consider helping with Father until I find someone. I have to be able to trust the person who cares for him."

The idea did not appeal to Lilly. "Clayton, you have been searching for over two months. I'm not sure Rebecca would consent to help." Although Lilly knew in her heart that Rebecca would be willing. Was it selfishness on Lilly's part?

At that point, Rebecca came from the kitchen to clear dishes from the table.

Lilly said, "Rebecca, Mr. Vello is going to leave next week. Mr. Lockwood wants to know if you would go to his place to take care of his father."

A pink glow started in the creamy complexion of Rebecca's pleasant face. Lilly had put her on the spot.

"I will pay you well," offered Clay.

Rebecca had never earned money of her own. In a quiet voice, she asked, "What do you think, Miss Lilly?"

"I think you should ask your brother." The decision was off Lilly's shoulders.

Clay rose from his chair. "I'll go out and have a talk with Josiah."

Tony made no effort to go with him. Rebecca continued with her chore. Lilly sat next to Tony feeling uncomfortable with his closeness.

"I should help Rebecca finish cleaning up," she said.

"No. Sit and talk to me. Clay told me about your husband and your little boy. I'm sorry. Now you're stuck with this place."

"Don't make me feel any sorrier for myself than I already feel," she said. "Why did you come here? I don't think it was just to help Clayton out."

He looked directly at her and smiled. "You're as wise as you are attractive. You're different than most women I've met. Truthfully, I had to get out of the city. When I received Clay's letter, the timing was perfect."

"I would call that taking advantage of a friend."

He shrugged a shoulder. "You may call it that. It has proved beneficial to both of us."

Lilly sighed. "I didn't mean to sound judgmental. Clayton hasn't had it easy either. He is a kind young man. He should be back at the university rather than to be saddled with his father and that big farm."

Tony nodded. "He's a good egg. I do have to return to New York next week. I have affairs that need to be settled. Lilly, would you ever consider

185

coming to New York for a weekend? There is so much to see and do. I know the city like the back of my hand. I'd be a great travel guide."

He dropped the Miss, but Lilly didn't seem to mind. She chuckled. "I haven't even been to Washington, D.C. I am not a traveler."

He took her hand. "It's time you got out to see what's over the hill. You can bring the girls and we will have a good time."

She pulled her hand from his. "No, I don't think so."

Clay was on his way back from talking to Josiah. He noticed Tony sitting too close to Lilly. Clay decided it was time for his friend to go back to New York. Mrs. Pierce wasn't up to the ways of city men, especially the slick ways of men like Anthony Vello.

Clay came to where they sat. "It's all set," he announced. "Josiah said it would be good for Rebecca to be out on her own and learn what it is to earn money."

Lilly was not joyous. Rebecca was her help and close companion during the long days. A wry look was sent in Clay's direction. "Will this be for a week, a month, or a year?"

She called, "Rebecca."

The young woman came out the back door. "Your brother agrees that it is fine for you to help Clayton with his father."

"Do you want me to go, Miss Lilly?"

"No I don't, but that might be selfish on my part." Lilly turned to Clayton. "Rebecca may come for no longer than a month. That should satisfy everyone."

Clay looked at the shy young woman. "Will you be ready on Friday?"

She nodded her head.

"Mrs. Pierce, thank you. Tony is leaving on the Friday morning train. I'll drive down that afternoon to get her."

Tony left his seat. "Think over what we talked about, Lilly."

Clay sent a quizzical look. He didn't care for Tony's casual use of her name. "I'll discuss buying the foal when I come for Rebecca," said Clay. "Chip will be looking for us, Tony. Did you have a good chat?"

"Nothing like setting some wheels in motion," Tony replied.

What did he mean by that?

In the quiet of her bedroom that night, Lilly thought about the tiring day. The wool would bring in some money and Josiah said there would be money from the lambs and sheep, enough money to buy a plow. She hated the constant battle of trying to keep herself on an even keel where money was concerned.

Her thoughts turned to Anthony Vello. She snickered to herself at the thought of going to the city for a weekend and spending it with him. She was sure he had plenty of money and would be more than happy to spend it on her. She could picture herself in a sharp hat and lace dress taking in the sights of the city she had seen in magazines. Lilly was not innocent. She knew Tony would expect something in return. No, money isn't everything. But wasn't it nice to be flirted with as though she wasn't a thirty-one year old widow?

Chapter 32

On Friday afternoon, Clay arrived at *Roseville* in his father's Model T. Rebecca was packed and waiting and nervous.

"Remember, Rebecca, Clayton said you may come back anytime you want. If you feel the need, you are to tell him. I know he has a lady who cooks and cleans so you won't have to do any of that. Your sole responsibility will be his father. I understand he can be difficult at times."

"I have taken care of older people." She smiled. "Although I don't want to be married to one."

Lilly gave her a hug. "And, that's how we all got together in the first place. Weren't we fortunate? You are like a daughter to me."

Clay was knocking on the kitchen door.

"Coming, Clayton," called Lilly.

Rebecca picked up her satchel and followed Lilly to the door.

Lilly opened it. "Good afternoon, Clayton. Did you get your friend to the train this morning?"

"Good afternoon. Tony is on his way." Clay looked at Rebecca. "I'll carry your satchel to the car."

She was reluctant to hand it to him.

"Go ahead," Lilly encouraged. "Clayton, this will be Rebecca's first trip in an automobile," she explained.

189

He smiled at the tall, solid, young woman with chestnut hair and deep brown eyes who stood next to Lilly. "This will be an adventure for you."

Rebecca wore a cream-colored wool cardigan over a blue-striped blouse and navy skirt. Her long hair was wound into a bun. She kissed Lilly on the cheek before she followed Clay to the car.

He opened the door for her and she stepped up into the car. She should have bent her head because she bumped it on the frame of the auto before she took her seat.

"I should have warned you," said Clay. "I always have to duck. Did you hurt yourself?"

She looked at him. "It wasn't a pleasant feeling. I will learn."

He opened the back door and set the satchel on the back seat. Clay went through the motions of starting the car before waving farewell to Lilly, who stood with a lost look on her face.

Rebecca felt the car move and tried to hang on to something but there was nothing there. She pressed her feet against the floor boards as the car made its way down the lane. She looked over and saw Clay had a wheel to hold on to.

Sensing her apprehension, Clay asked, "What are you thinking?"

She faced straight ahead. "I am thinking that this car should have some reins."

He laughed. "You'll get used to it."

Rebecca had been on the road to Berryville when Lilly brought her to and from Addie's. Now, with the spring grass, the redwoods, and dogwoods in bloom, she was in awe of the natural beauty.

"Mrs. Pierce says that you and Josiah are from the Amish country."

Clay's deep voice startled her. "*Ya.* I mean yes."

"Did you come to be with your brother?"

"Yes."

"How do you like living with Mrs. Pierce? Do you miss your home?" Clay was doing his best to make conversation.

"It is different here, but I am happy to be with Josiah, Miss Lilly and her girls. It makes me feel at home."

"Rebecca, thank you for agreeing to come. I will keep my word that you can return at any time. Don't be shy about telling me if you want to leave. My father can be difficult. Even with Tony, I sometimes had to help. When he gets in that state, he is strong and it took the two of us to handle him so he wouldn't hurt himself."

Clay turned onto the main street of Berryville. "We have plenty of stores for whatever you need."

She looked over at him. "Mr. Lockwood, I come from plain people. We are used to making do with what we have, but if there is something I need, I will ask."

"Do you think we could be on a first name basis? I would like to call you Rebecca and not have it sound like you are a servant. More like friends. You will call me Clay."

She thought about it and silently said the names. "That is comfortable for me."

He almost breathed a sigh of relief. "That is comfortable for me too, Rebecca."

She smiled as she watched his big hands turn the wheel onto a lane that led up to a big white farmhouse. Clay parked the Model T to the side. "We'll go in through the kitchen. I'll introduce you to Faith."

He stopped the car and came over to open the door for Rebecca. "Watch your head," he warned.

She touched her forehead. "I remember."

Clay held her hand as she stepped down from the car. It was a warm and gentle touch. She stood next to this tall, brawny man showing a wide smile and black hair fringing under his driver's cap. He was a few inches taller than Rebecca.

"It is nice to look up to a man," she said. "Many times I am taller than they are or we are at eye level."

He opened the back door to retrieve her satchel. "I think I understand. Many times I tower over women and some men. I was the klutzy kid when I was young."

"Ah," she agreed. "It took me some time to grow into myself."

"Rebecca, I think we are going to get along just fine. Let's go in and meet Faith."

She nodded. The earlier tension she felt was gone.

The small black woman was bustling around the kitchen. She looked up at both of them when they came in the door.

"Mister Clay. It's good you got here when you did. I'll have supper ready in a half-hour and I don't want it tastin' old by sittin' on the stove."

"Faith, this is Miss Rebecca. She will be taking care of Father."

"Well, you come right on in young lady. You sure do be tall."

Faith said to Clay, "Chip be chaffin' at the bit to git on home. He say your father be sleepin' mos' of the time an' he be bored sittin' there."

"I don't blame him," replied Clay. "I remember what it was like to be a teenager."

Rebecca smiled. *"Rumschpringe,"* said Rebecca.

Clay was puzzled.

"It means running around in Amish."

Clay laughed. "You remember teenage years also. Sometimes I wish I was still in them. Carefree days."

"For some," answered Rebecca. "I am glad to be twenty-one soon."

"Come along. I'll show you the room you will be using and we can peek in on my father."

Rebecca followed Clay through the dining room and parlor. He opened the door to her room and placed the satchel on the floor next to the twin cherry bed. "This small door connects with my father's room. We'll go through."

Chip jumped up from the chair when they entered. "I almost fell asleep."

"This is Rebecca. She will be staying here to help."

"Hi, Rebecca," Chip greeted her. "He's been sleeping all day so he'll probably keep you awake all night."

Rebecca walked to the bedside to see the gray-haired man she was to care for. She felt she would not have much difficulty with him.

Clay informed, "Chip, there's an envelope on the dining room table for you. Be sure and pick it up on your way out."

"Thanks. Are you going to be needing me again?"

"I don't think so."

"See you later," said Chip, and hurried out the door.

"Rebecca, once you get settled, we'll have supper in the dining room."

"What about your father? When does he eat?"

"Tony used to bring a tray in and feed him in here."

"Clay." It was the first time she had called him by name. "If I am to sit in the dining room, your father should too."

Clay brushed the suggestion away with the wave of his hand. "I'm not sure it would make any difference to Father. Most of the time he doesn't know where he is."

She shook her head. "It won't be long before it is time to eat. I'll put my things away and wake him up. Can he walk?"

"There is a wheelchair but we don't use it."

"Then you and I will help him come to the table. I believe it is better to be out of bed. We can pull the wheelchair up to the table."

"He will just make a mess."

"I will clean it up," she countered. "He has been in his room all day. How would you feel if you were in one room all day?"

Clay wagged his head. "Rebecca, I can see you have a mind of your own."

"It is the Amish way," she said.

Clay wasn't so sure.

Chapter 33

Rebecca had been gone three weeks. Lilly missed her company and wondered how she was doing. Lilly could have telephoned, but she didn't want it to seem as though she were prying. Josiah said all must be going well because they hadn't heard otherwise.

Lilly and Josiah were sitting and finishing breakfast.

"I'd like to go and see for myself," she said. "I believe you should go with me and talk with Alex about those cattle of his. We can stop and see Rebecca and say hello to Laura."

Josiah stood and took his cup to the stove for more hot coffee. "I've got that plowing to finish and put in the crops. That new plow is a dandy."

Lilly smiled. "It's good Clayton bought that foal he wanted. It paid for the plow and the seed."

He came back to the table. "Too bad you couldn't have held onto that foal for a while, he might have brought a better price."

Lilly shrugged a shoulder. "I have to pay the bills. I'm happy Clayton bought him."

"Give me two days to finish," Josiah said. "Then we can go up and see about the cattle."

"Can I help you?" asked Lilly.

He raised his eyebrows. "Do you know how to sow corn?"

Lilly was almost sorry she had offered. She had never had to sow corn. She wanted to see Rebecca, Addie and Laura. If planting corn would help get her there, she would do it.

"We'll go on Saturday," Lilly told him. "That way Emily and Flossie can go, and it will give one more day for you to finish whatever you need to do."

Saturday also gave Lilly one more day to prepare. She knew Rebecca's birthday was that week. She had gone into the department store in Boyce and bought material for a pretty apron. It was finished except for red rick-rack around the pocket and the neck. The material was red-checked cloth that would be pretty over Rebecca's blue dress, which Lilly knew was her favorite one to wear. Lilly also baked a spice cake. The cake she would give to Laura.

Josiah was ready to leave. "If you want to learn how to sow the corn, follow me out to the barn. I'll show you how to use the corn planter. There's a patch on the north side that has been plowed and harrowed."

Lilly followed him out. The corn planter was a piece of wood about five inches wide and three feet long with a metal point at one end and a handle on the other. There was a metal cylinder on the front of the board and a metal lever that opened and closed the cylinder. Josiah filled the cylinder with kernels of corn, drove the point into the ground and pulled the lever that released three kernels at a time.

197

"One to grow, one for the birds, and one for insurance," he said. "You could use the hoe and put the corn in by hand but you would have to cover them over with dirt. This way they are deep enough and it saves time."

The metal contraption was awkward. He handed it to Lilly and watched as she mimicked what he had shown her. This was not going to be easy, but she was determined.

"Are you sure you want to do this?" asked Josiah.

She looked him square in the eye. "I'm sure all the Amish women sow corn."

He smiled. "They do. They are used to farming work."

Lilly stood back and put a hand on her hip. "If the Amish women can do it, then so can I."

That half-smile appeared on his face. "I'll be getting to the plowing. You can start whenever you want."

Lilly went back to the house to put on barn shoes and work gloves and back she went. She lifted the corn planter by its handle, jabbed it into the soft dirt and pulled the lever. A few jabs into the ground and the pull of the lever let her know her shoulders and back would hurt by evening. She worked until it was time to get supper. When she finished, Lilly wiped the perspiration from her face with the back side of her soiled apron, stood back and admired her work.

After supper, Emily and Flossie helped wash the dishes before they did their homework for school. When they finished she sent them up to bed. She put three pots of water on the stove and heated water for a bath to soak her aching body or she wouldn't be able to move in the morning.

Once supper was over and before Josiah returned to his room above the porch, he placed a bottle of horse liniment on the table. "You might need this," he said.

Lilly just looked at him.

She took her bath and, horse liniment or not, she rubbed it into her painful shoulders and aching legs. She wished someone was there to soothe it onto her back. A little voice in her head reminded her that if Frank were here, he could do it even with his rough, calloused hands. And, if Frank were here she wouldn't be out sowing corn. For seven long months Lilly Pierce had been on her own and she didn't like it.

Chapter 34

On Saturday, Emily and Flossie dressed up to go visiting. They wanted to bring Ef. Josiah said if it was all right with their mother, he didn't see any reason the dog couldn't come along.

"Ef will be your responsibility," Lilly told Josiah.

It was a pleasant May day. Lilly took a jug of water and sandwiches. She packed the spice cake carefully and wrapped the box containing Rebecca's apron with flowered wrapping paper and secured the package with red yarn. Emily and Flossie had made the birthday card by cutting out a picture of birds in a flowering tree they found in a magazine. They pasted it onto a piece of paper then folded the paper into a square. Inside, they wrote: *Happy Birthday, Rebecca. Please come back to Roseville. From Emily, Flossie, Momma, Josiah, and Ef.*

They showed it to Lilly before they slipped it under the yarn tied around the package. Lilly wasn't sure they were the best chosen words but she made no remark.

Josiah hitched Jack up to the buggy and drove to the house. Emily and Flossie climbed into the back seat with Ef between them. Lilly put the jug of water, the picnic basket of sandwiches, and the spice cake in the back of the buggy.

"Don't let the dog get your dresses dirty," Lilly cautioned before she stepped up to take a seat beside Josiah. "And don't let her get into the picnic basket or the cake. I think they are safe behind you. Emily, hold onto Ef's leash. She might take a notion to jump after a rabbit or something."

Then Lilly got out of the buggy and went back into the house to get a blanket. "We might need this," she said. "Girls don't let the dog get near Rebecca's present."

Josiah had been patient. "Do you want to leave Ef here, Miss Lilly?"

"Well, certainly not. Go ahead. Let's get started."

Jack was in good form. They made it to *Lockwood* in less than two hours. It was ten in the morning when Josiah guided Jack up the long lane that led to the house.

Addie came hurrying out the back door to greet them. "I am so glad you are here." She hugged the girls and Lilly, who flinched at the tight hug. "Are you all right, Aunt Lilly?"

"Momma's been out sowing corn," said Emily.

Lilly sent a cautioning look at her eldest daughter.

Aunt Lilly sowing corn? A baffling look crossed Addie's face. She knew better than to say any more. "Alex is out at the barn."

"Addie, have you met Josiah?"

She offered a welcoming smile. "Yes, briefly. It is nice to see you again."

He touched the light straw hat he wore, "Thank you, Mrs. Lockwood. I'll go on to the barn, Miss Lilly." Josiah tapped the reins.

"Come inside. Ella has fried doughnuts for you."

Lilly, Addie and the girls sat at the kitchen table. Ella poured each a glass of cold milk and placed dessert plates and a platter of doughnuts on the table.

"Ella won't be with us much longer. She and Charlie are going to be married in September."

"That's wonderful," Lilly said. "Where will they live?"

"On Clay's place. Charlie says he likes working with horses better than cows. Alex has been in a bind since Jess left. Jess could handle those heavy cattle of ours. Most of the men he's talked to either want dairy cows or horses."

"Josiah is out there checking to see if the cattle are a good investment for me."

"I wouldn't take Josiah for Rebecca's brother. They don't look anything alike," said Addie. "I like his looks. How is he working out?"

"I would be lost without him," admitted Lilly. "He needs another man to help him, but I can't afford it right now. As it is, I am keeping my head above water."

"What does that mean?" asked Flossie.

"It's a figure of speech," answered Lilly, which seemed to satisfy her young daughter.

Emily was busy eating doughnuts.

"How would you two like to go see Miss Lottie and her baby?" questioned Addie.

Two sets of ears perked up.

"They have been asking when they could see the baby," said Lilly. "Is it fine with Lottie?"

Addie nodded. "I checked with her yesterday. She said she would love to have company and show off Baby Jess."

On the way to Lottie's, the girls skipped along, Lilly and Addie talked.

"We are making a day of it," said Lilly. "After we leave here we are going to see Rebecca and stop in at your mother's house."

"Clay told Alex that he is pleased to have Rebecca there. He said she is good with Mr. Lockwood. She is able to calm him when he gets rambunctious, which others haven't been able to do."

"I miss her," Lilly admitted. "I miss her cheery company and her help. Josiah says it is good for her to be away on her own and earning money."

"Aunt Lilly, you seem to put a lot of trust in Josiah. He is a hired man."

"Yes, he is. He is trustworthy and has a good head on his shoulders. He knows more about running the farm than I do. I don't look at him as a hired man. He is on a par with me."

"Maybe he is like Jess," mused Addie. "Jess was educated, but he loved the hands on work. The best thing I did for him was to introduce him to my friend, Fannie. I don't know if they will ever come back East."

Addie knocked on Lottie's door.

The four of them quietly entered the living room where Lottie had placed the baby's cradle. Little Cal clung to her skirt so she picked him up. "You know Addie," Lottie said to him. "And this is Miss Lilly, Emily and Flossie."

Two button eyes looked at them.

"He'll be fine in a couple of minutes. He's shy at first. When he gets comfortable he'll start to show off and want all the attention. You came at the right time. I just fed the baby and he's still awake."

Lottie walked to the cradle and the others followed. Lottie put Little Cal down and picked up Baby Jess. She leaned down so the girls could see the quiet bundle in her arms.

"He's little," observed Emily.

"He looks like a baby doll," said Flossie.

Lottie smiled. "He has a loud cry when he's hungry."

"He is beautiful. May I hold him?" asked Lilly.

"Of course," said Lottie as she placed the baby in Lilly's arms.

A lump rose in Lilly's throat. She hadn't held a baby since Carroll Joseph. Had it been over two years since her little CJ died? Lilly didn't speak, she rocked the baby in her arms before she handed him back to his mother.

Addie sensed her aunt's instant melancholia. She said to Lottie, "Aunt Lilly is going to visit Momma before they go back to Boyce. Do you want her to take anything to your mother when they go?"

Lottie was placing the baby back in his cradle. "No, I can't think of anything. Did you drive the girls up, Miss Lilly?"

"No. Josiah, the man who works for me. He drove us up so he can check out the cattle Alex is so enthused about."

"Where are my manners? Won't you sit down?" said Lottie.

At that moment a ball came rolling over Lilly's foot. "I wish we could stay. It looks like the girls and Little Cal are beginning to enjoy each other's company. We have to look in on Josiah's sister and visit at Laura's."

"Addie told me his sister is caring for Mr. Lockwood. Poor Clay, I think he gets overwhelmed. Did you meet his friend from New York City, Miss Lilly?"

Addie intercepted. " I wasn't comfortable with that Anthony Vello. He was too smooth. Fannie pointed out those kinds of men when I lived in Washington."

Lilly nodded but didn't say a word. What would these young girls think if they knew Tony had invited her to New York City for a weekend? She smiled to herself. After sowing a patch of corn a weekend in New York City with Tony Vello didn't sound half bad.

They left Lottie's and walked to the barn where Lilly saw the two cows and one bull Alex said would be a good start. The cows looked twice the size of her milking cow. He said he would give her a good price and she could pay in installments.

"That isn't the bull that almost did Jess in, is it?" she asked.

Alex assured her it wasn't.

Lilly told him she would have to think it over.

Josiah snapped his fingers and Ef hopped up into the buggy. The girls jumped into the back seat and Lilly took her place in front. They were off.

Chapter 35

Rebecca burst into tears when they arrived at Clay's place and the girls handed her the present. She kissed all four of them, "I am so happy to see you."

Clay came out of the room he used as an office. "I wondered what the commotion was about."

"Look, Clay. They have given me a beautiful apron for my birthday."

Clay? Lilly and Josiah exchanged a glance.

Clay warmly greeted Lilly and the girls and shook Josiah's hand. "It's good to have you here. Rebecca is not one to complain, but I know she misses all of you."

Lilly noticed that the earlier stress she had seen in Clay's face was gone. "How is your father?"

"Sleeping more, eating less. Overall he seems to be more comfortable under Rebecca's care."

"It is much like caring for a baby," said Rebecca. "Rubbing his shoulders and his back and singing softly helps to drive away the demons that torment him at times."

"Come in and sit in the parlor. Father is asleep. Tell us what has been going on at the farm," said Clay.

Lilly and Josiah sat on green velvet chairs. The girls sat on brown leather footstools. Clay and Rebecca sat together on a beige settee with a background of the fox hunt.

"We brought Ef with us," said Flossie. "She's out in the buggy. Do you want to see her?"

"I will be glad to see her before you leave."

"Mister Clay, how long does Rebecca have to stay here?" asked Emily. "We want her to come home."

"Emily, don't be impolite," cautioned her mother. Although Lilly wanted to know too.

Clay looked at Rebecca and they smiled at each other. "Rebecca may leave anytime she wants to."

"I will stay until Mr. Lockwood no longer needs me," Rebecca informed. "I don't know how long that will be."

Lilly looked at the two of them sitting side by side and thought it would be wise for Rebecca to return soon. "We came to check out the cattle Alex thinks I need," Lilly said. "Josiah is a better judge of that than I am."

"What do you think?" Clay asked Josiah.

"It will take another man to help me. Miss Lilly and I haven't talked about whether that is the way to go."

"This business of raising horses is proving more difficult than I thought," Clay said, "I'm trying to get Tony Vello interested in buying into a few horses."

"Whatever would your friend know about raising horses?" Lilly blurt out.

Clay leaned forward in his seat. "He spends time around the big race tracks. He knows a lot of the owners. I think he could be a good connection, especially if he is part owner in a horse."

Clay leaned back with a sigh. "I've got to find some way to keep this place afloat."

Josiah inquired, "How is the foal you bought from Miss Lilly? I'd like to see him."

"Let's take a walk out. I'll check out *Ef* and you can check out *Fortune*."

"Is that what you call the foal? That's a funny name," said Flossie.

Clay winked and ruffled her blonde curls with his large hand as he rose from the settee. "That's what I hope he will bring me," he said.

Lilly and Rebecca stayed behind.

"Rebecca, I have been concerned. Do you truly like being here?"

Her reply was enthusiastic. "Oh, Miss Lilly, I do."

"You seem to be comfortable with Clayton."

Lilly noticed a delicate pink rise in Rebecca's face. "I am. He is kind and helpful. He said for my birthday he will take me to the cinema."

The words jolted Lilly. "What about Mr. Lockwood? Who will look after him?"

"Chip. It will be less than two hours."

Lilly sat and thought. "Have you ever been to a cinema?"

"Clay says it will be a funny one. Something about some silly policemen. He said I need to get away from the house and get some fresh air."

"Rebecca, if you go with Clayton, it might start rumors."

"You mean about me being a single woman taking care of Clay's father and living in the same house as Clay?"

Now Lilly's face flushed. "Something like that."

"As long as I know in my heart that I am pure, I don't care what others say, Miss Lilly. Amish or English, it is the same."

"I'm sorry, Rebecca. You are right." Lilly stood. "I do have to go because we need to be back for evening chores, and I still have to go to my sister's house." She hugged Rebecca and hated to leave without her.

"I like Miss Laura, although she is not one to smile much."

Lilly defended her only sister. "Life hasn't been easy for her."

"Is life easy for any of us? You have had your sorrows."

Lilly hugged her again. How astute this young woman is. "I feel so much better now that I have seen you are doing well," Lilly said. "I hope it won't be too much longer before you come back to our home for good."

Lilly walked out to the buggy. Clay, Josiah and the girls were coming back from the barn with Ef at their heels.

Emily and Flossie ran to their mother.

"Momma, you should see how beautiful the foal is. I wish we had kept him."

So do I, thought Lilly. Especially since Josiah said he might bring a better price. She sighed before she climbed up onto the seat. The girls got into the back and Josiah shook Clay's hand.

Lilly waved. "Good-bye, Clayton. Take good care of our Rebecca."

A wide smile spread across his face. "That's a promise, Mrs. Pierce."

Josiah chucked to Jack and they were on their way to John and Laura Richards' house.

"What do you think, Josiah?" asked Lilly.

"About what?"

"About your sister? Do you think all is going the way it should?"

He looked over at her with that sly smile of his. "I believe all is going better than I thought it would."

What did he mean by that? Lilly didn't ask.

Laura and John were pleased to see Lilly and the girls. It was the first time John had met Lilly's hired man. Now everyone close to Lilly had met Josiah. Why was that important? Lilly wasn't exactly sure but she felt it was.

She assured both Laura and John that all was going well at *Roseville*. It wouldn't do to let them know she was concerned about money.

They all stood in the yard. Laura wanted them to come into the house and have a piece of the cake Lilly had brought.

"Rebecca's birthday is tomorrow, perhaps you can share it with her. I am sorry we can't stay. As it is we will have to hurry back to get the evening chores done," said Lilly.

They drove back through Berryville and headed for Boyce.

"You did pack sandwiches didn't you, Miss Lilly?" said Josiah.

"Yes, I have sandwiches and also cookies."

"It's such a pretty day, why don't we stop at the cemetery at Old Chapel. There's a big fir tree where we can spread the blanket and have a picnic," he suggested.

"A picnic in a cemetery?" questioned Lilly.

"It will be quiet."

Lilly laughed aloud. "It will be that. Will this cause you to be too much behind with the evening work?"

"I'll bet that if I mention a picnic to the girls, they will be more than happy to spread some hay around for me."

Lilly smiled at him. "As long as they don't have to muck out stalls."

He said, "It will give Jack a rest and be a perfect ending to a full and enjoyable day."

"Did you enjoy yourself, Josiah?"

"More than I have in a long time," he answered.

Chapter 36

With money from the sale of wool and market sheep and lambs, Lilly was able to put money into savings. She knew she would need it for the winter months when there would be little money coming in. The bills didn't stop, and she still had to pay on the mortgage at the bank. She could pay a few months ahead although she decided it wise to keep the money. Who can predict what the summer will bring. Maybe hay and feed will be scarce because of lack of rain or crops ruined because of too much rain. Tony Vello was right. Farming is a risky business.

Josiah suggested she buy the two cows Alex offered as long as they were bred. She could wait on a bull. He said he could handle the cows by himself, but not if the bull came too. Lilly would pay Alex for the proper feed mixture and Josiah would bring it from *Lockwood* in the wagon. She hoped Josiah was right. What did she know about raising big fat cows!

The wagon was aging and Lilly knew she couldn't spare the expense of a new one. She added it to her list of prayers even though she wasn't sure it was proper to ask for a wagon to remain workable. The Lord had enough to do than worry about an aging farm wagon.

It was three weeks after their visit to Berryville. The girls were in school and Josiah had taken the dog with him to work in the fields. Lilly took a bag of peas a friend at church had given to her and went to sit under the shade of an oak tree.

She was shelling the peas into a bowl when she saw a car turn into the drive. It looked like the Model T Clayton drives, but most of those cars look the same. She sat on the bench until the auto stopped and her heart jumped into her throat when the driver got out. Anthony Vello!

He wore a boater hat, beige pants and a beige shirt open at the neck with a silk cravat. The outfit made him look impressive with his dark hair and olive skin. The diamond ring was still on his fifth finger. He carried a bouquet of violets in a small lavender-colored glass vase.

His smile drew her in. "Hello, Lilly. These are to brighten your day."

She was frozen in her spot. "Hello, Tony." Did it sound as uptight as she felt? She reached for the vase and admired the violets before she set it on a stump next to the bench.

"Surprised to see me?"

She could only nod.

"Clay wanted me to come see his horses. I brought a man who knows his stuff to tell me if they are worth an investment. We're staying at the hotel in Berryville."

Lilly relaxed enough to find her voice. "I certainly didn't expect to see you. Thank you for the flowers. Did you settle your affairs in New York City?"

He came and sat next to her on the bench. She left the bowl of peas between them.

"It cost me a bundle. I'm even."

Lilly wasn't sure what that meant and she didn't care. Neither Clay nor Tony had said why he came the first time. Caring for Mr. Lockwood sounded like a good excuse.

"How long will you be staying?"

"Just a couple of days. I came to see if you have changed your mind about coming up to the city for a weekend."

She shook her head.

"You can bring the girls. Rebecca can come too. It would be educational for them."

Lilly laughed aloud. "I'm sure it would. You must know that Rebecca is taking care of Clayton's father."

Tony leaned back against the bench and crossed his ankles. "I'll be surprised if the old man makes it through next week."

"What makes you say that?"

"I took care of a lot of guys in the hospital when I was in the service. When their breathing sounds like his, they weren't long for this world."

They sat in silence.

"You've got a pleasant spot here, Lilly."

"Yes, I have."

"Would you come if Clay and Rebecca came along?" He was back to New York City.

"Clayton and Rebecca? I doubt Clayton would even consider such a proposition."

"Don't bet your farm on it. He's sweet on that young lady."

That wasn't surprising news to Lilly. She had seen the way Clay looked at Rebecca. "What exactly do you want, Tony?"

He uncrossed his ankles and shifted his body to look at her. "You're the first true lady I've met. You're too young to be a widow and having to struggle day to day with this farm. Wouldn't you like to get away for a carefree two days? I promise to act the gentleman. I want you to see what New York offers. I want you to get to know me."

Lilly sat for a moment. "Don't think I didn't consider the idea when you first suggested it. I feel like I have aged ten years in the seven months Frank has been gone. Sometimes I have to remind myself I was married. I am supposed to be in mourning for at least a year. I think I have been in mourning since my little CJ died."

She stopped and looked squarely at him. "You don't know how many times I have wished to get on that train that comes through here and ride off into oblivion."

She pressed her fingers to her lips. "I shouldn't have told you that. I don't know why I did."

He reached for her hand. "Come on, Lilly. It's only for two days. You can leave the girls with your sister or at Addie's. I'll pass it by Clay. Once he doesn't have the responsibility of his father both he and Rebecca will need some spirit-lifting time."

Anthony Vello was convincing. His hand in hers felt warm and smooth not the calloused rough farm hands she had known.

She pulled her hand from his. "I promise I will think about it."

He dashed her with his smile once again. "I won't ask for more. When the time comes, I will make all the arrangements for the four of us."

"It won't be proper for you to pick up the expense."

He waved her statement away. "I owe it to Clay. He helped me out of a jam. You give me something to look forward to and Rebecca is your insurance if you are worried about your reputation. It will be you, Clay and Rebecca leaving from here. No one will know about me. Three people who need to get away for a couple of days because of the strain of the last year."

Lilly was beginning to see how Tony acquired the nickname, Slick.

"Would you care for a cup of tea?"

"No thanks. I've got to get Clay's car back."

Lilly stood, careful not to upset the bowl of peas. She walked him to the car. "I'm glad you came by, Tony. Good luck with getting into the horse business."

"In a few weeks, I will see you in New York." He reached for her hand and brought her fingers to his lips. "Good-bye, Lilly."

She couldn't speak. She waved as the car went down the drive. Lilly Pierce was in a state of confusion.

Josiah Bly watched from the barn.

Chapter 37

Tony was right. Old Mr. Lockwood passed away within the week. Addie wanted to have the funeral dinner at *Lockwood*, but Clay and Alex both said their father was to be buried on the farm that was his home and the funeral dinner would be held there. That being the case, Addie said Ella would go and help Faith because it would be too much for Faith to prepare without help. Mr. Lockwood was well known in Clarke County and surrounding areas. There would be a large turnout.

The funeral was held on Saturday. It was warm with a slight breeze. A lovely day to be buried, if there is ever a good day to be buried.

Lilly had the girls dress in their Sunday best. She wore the black dress she had worn when she buried CJ and Frank. It was a heavy taffeta, too warm for May but appropriate for the funeral. She had to buy a summer hat, which cost her $4.89, a necessary expense. She settled for a black straw with one side turned up and held by a tasteful pin made out of a peacock feather. She asked Josiah if he wanted to go to the funeral.

"I believe I should out of respect for Clay, although I didn't know his father. And, it doesn't seem right for you to have to drive the girls. I will come."

Lilly heaved a sigh of relief. She didn't want to have to hassle with the horse and buggy wearing her good clothes.

Josiah drove Jack and the buggy to the back of the house. Lilly had never seen him wearing a suit. He was dressed in black with a white shirt and string tie. His hat was a black Fedora. Collar-length blonde hair shone under the hat as did the blue of his eyes. Lilly took a second look.

"Are you and the girls ready, Miss Lilly? We should be on our way."

"I wish Ef didn't have to stay here," sighed Flossie.

"We can't very well take her to a funeral," said Lilly.

"She has a nice spot in on the side porch where she likes to sleep," said Josiah. "Think how happy she'll be when we come back home."

He tapped the reins and they were on their way to Berryville.

The funeral service was held outdoors with the reverend from the Episcopal church presiding. The John. H. Enders Funeral Service handled the burial in Mr. Lockwood's favorite spot on the farm.

Funerals are always full of mixed feelings. For Clay, his were sadness and relief. For the past six months, ever since he had returned from the service, his father was not the man he remembered. He had not been his father's favorite son but they had good times together. He decided to concentrate on those memories.

After the interment, food was set out on long tables under the trees. Chairs were available for those in need. Men stood in groups and women came prepared with blankets they spread on the ground. Rebecca, Laura, and Lottie's mother helped with the serving.

Alex and Addie greeted those who came. Addie had always been the helper. Now she was the wife of a landowner her role had changed.

Josiah stood with John Richards, Caleb Dunn, and Lottie's father. Probably a group who knew more about farming than the men who owned the big estates.

Lottie came with her two little ones. "Mrs. Pierce, do you mind if I spread my blanket next to yours?"

"I would love it," answered Lilly.

"Emily and Flossie help me and Miss Lottie spread the blankets then you can go and fill your plates."

The girls did as they were asked and wanted a peek at the baby before they left for the food.

Lilly offered, "Lottie, I'll hold Baby Jess while you get Little Cal and yourself something to eat."

"I would appreciate that. He most likely won't eat more than a piece of fried chicken and a few bites of potato. When he's outdoors he wants to run and play."

Lilly smiled. "That's what little boys are supposed to do. The girls can watch him after they eat. It won't take long for this somber group to lighten up. Once the children start to play and wine is served, the mood will change."

Lottie laughed. "I hope my mother keeps an eye on how much my father takes in. He likes his alcohol. The Talleys are here to put an article in the *Courier*. I wouldn't want my father to be front page news."

"Mr. Talley is here to cover the funeral, Lavinia is here to dig up whatever she can."

Lottie looked up. "Mrs. Pierce, you surprise me."

"Sometimes I surprise myself," said Lilly.

Emily and Flossie returned with full plates. Lottie fed Little Cal and herself. Lilly was pleased to sit and hold the sleeping baby in her arm.

When they were finished, Emily and Flossie took the toddler with them to play with Sarah Jane and other children attending.

"If he's too much trouble, bring him back to me," Lottie told the girls.

"Stay in sight," cautioned Lilly.

"We will," replied Emily. Off they went to play.

"You had better get your food before it's gone," said Lottie. "There are a lot of people here."

Lilly got up from the blanket and waited for her legs to feel stable. She had been sitting Indian style for too long.

Rebecca was putting another platter of ham on the table. Her smile was wide when she saw Lilly. "Miss Lilly, I am so happy to see you. I saw Josiah and the girls."

"How are you doing, Rebecca?"

"The last few days have been difficult. It is a sad time for Clay."

"When will you be coming back to *Roseville?*"

"I am planning for the day after tomorrow. I will stay and help clean up and clear up what needs to be done."

"Do you want me to come and fetch you back?"

"No. Clay said he will drive me."

Lilly wanted to ask her about Clay but there were others around. Lilly would talk to Rebecca when she returned home.

Lilly took her plate of food back to the blanket. Lottie was busy with the baby and keeping an eye on the children to be sure her little one didn't wander away.

Lillie's thoughts drifted to New York City and Anthony Vello. He had disturbed her world. Would she feel guilty if she went? Would she rue her decision not to take this opportunity? What would Addie say? What would Laura say? The thoughts caused her mind to halt. It occurred to her that Laura was the one to ask, but not today. Lilly would set a time to come to Berryville.

Lottie had packed up and left. It had been a couple of hours before Josiah came to ask Lilly if she was ready to go. He no sooner came to her side when Lavinia Talley waddled up.

"Lilly, I haven't been able to get over here to talk to you. There are so many important people at this gathering."

"Hello, Mrs. Talley. This is Josiah Bly. He takes care of my farm. Josiah, Mrs. Talley's husband is editor of the weekly paper."

Lavinia took him in from head to toe.

He gave her his delightful smile and tipped his hat.

Lavinia twittered. "How fortunate that you have found help, Lilly. How is your farm prospering? It has to be a monumental task after the sudden loss of your husband." Without taking a breath she addressed Josiah, "I understand you are not from around here and you were the driver for the Caldwells. There must have been something that drew you to Lilly's place."

"Love of animals, Mrs. Talley. Are you ready to go, Mrs. Pierce?"

Brushoffs didn't faze Lavinia. She merely turned and waddled away.

Lilly finished folding the blanket she was holding. "I will have to get the girls."

Josiah took the blanket from her. Together they went to get Emily and Flossie.

"Do we have to go now? We want to play another game," complained Emily.

"I'm sorry," said Lilly. "I wish we could stay but there are chores to do once we get home."

With reluctance the girls said good-bye to their new-found friends and walked to where Jack and the buggy waited. Lilly went to say a word to Clayton. He was standing by himself.

"Clayton, I am sorry for the loss of your father."

"Thank you, Mrs. Pierce."

"Rebecca says she will be returning in two days."

Clay nodded. "I will drive her home. This will be a lonely place without her."

"I understand loneliness, Clayton. You will stay for lunch when you bring her home?"

"I will."

Lilly went to the buggy. Josiah's strong grip guided her up.

"Don't worry about Clay," he said in a quiet voice. "He will be fine."

Chapter 38

Rebecca was to arrive around noontime. Lilly didn't tell the girls because they would want to stay home from school. It was early June and there were few school days left.

Lilly sang to herself as she busied around the kitchen. She made a chicken pot pie, baked bread, and apple cobbler. Because it was a special occasion, she laid her best linen tablecloth and china on the dining room table. Josiah would be in his work clothes but even that was fine with her. She knew Rebecca would be pleased to have her brother there.

The Model T came up the drive and parked behind the house. Clay opened the door for Rebecca and carried the satchel Lilly had lent her.

Lilly was out the door in a flash and hugged Rebecca. "It's good to have you home. Hello, Clayton."

"Hello, Mrs. Pierce. Here she is safe and sound just as I promised."

Lilly looked past them. "Here comes Josiah. He must have heard the car."

Rebecca ran to meet him. He put his arm around her as they came to where Lilly and Clay waited.

Josiah shook Clay's hand. "Thank you for bringing my sister back."

"You're welcome."

"I have the lunch ready," informed Lilly. "Josiah, once you wash up we will eat."

The three went into the house while Josiah washed his face and hands at the outdoor well.

"Miss Lilly, how beautiful the table looks. We are going to eat in the dining room?" said a pleased Rebecca.

"Because it is a special day."

"What special day is that?"

Lilly smiled. "The day you have come back to us."

A broad smile appeared on Rebecca's fair face. "You are too *gut* to me. I mean good."

Lilly chuckled. "Take your places and I'll bring the pot pie and the tea."

"I will help," said Rebecca.

"This is your homecoming. You are not to work today."

"Rebecca has worked hard since she came to take care of Father. After Tony and I struggled with him, I was afraid she wouldn't be able to handle him. She was a calming influence." Clay looked at Rebecca. "And on me," he added.

A delicate pink came to her cheeks.

Lilly sensed Rebecca's discomfiture. "Does everyone want tea?"

Tea was the choice. Lilly dished out the chicken pot pie while the bread and butter were passed.

"I have missed Emily and Flossie. Are they doing well in school?" Rebecca asked.

"They are. I didn't dare tell them you would be back today or they would hound me to death to stay home."

"I believe Ef has grown twice the size as when I left," Rebecca observed.

"Mrs. Pierce, I told you she would be a good dog for you," said Clay.

"I think she has adopted Josiah or he has adopted her," said Lilly. "She used to be under my feet before he came."

"She's a farm dog and she needs to be used as one," said Josiah. "Ef comes in the house every evening and she is through with me then."

Lilly laughed, "That's because I feed her well."

"And let her sleep in your room," added Josiah.

It was Lilly's turn to blush. "She was lonesome by herself."

Rebecca agreed, "*Ya*, Miss Lilly, Ef does love you."

"I hear you are buying two of Alex's cows," said Clay.

"Josiah says he thinks it is the thing to do. I will buy the bull later, once I can afford to hire another man."

"I'm sure you remember Tony Vello, Mrs. Pierce. He came down over a week ago and brought a knowledgeable horse man with him," said Clay. "I'm hoping they will want to invest in one or more of my horses."

So, Tony Vello didn't say a word to Clay about coming to see Lilly. Josiah raised an eyebrow and Lilly was quiet.

She questioned, "If they are interested in your horses, how will investment help unless they buy them?"

"I'm not sure. Tony says if they can be race horses, everyone shares in the profits. I look for ways to make money. If I had my way, I'd let John Richards run the place. Addie could do the books. I could go back to the university. In a few years I could open my own drugstore."

"Have you discussed this with Alex?" asked Lilly.

"He's not encouraging."

"You have to do what is right for you, Clayton," advised Lilly. "Is everyone ready for coconut cake? I baked it especially for Rebecca's homecoming."

That suggestion was welcomed.

After lunch was over Clay was ready to head back to Berryville. Josiah shook his hand and headed in the direction of the north field. He whistled to Ef and the dog went running to join him.

Lilly and Rebecca stood by the car. Lilly hugged Clay and told him he was welcome to come back anytime. She turned and went into the house.

Rebecca stood in her place.

Lilly watched from the kitchen window where she saw Clay take Rebecca's hand. She couldn't hear the words but she could see there was a mutual understanding between them. Rebecca stood back from the car and waved as he puttered away. Lilly watched as the former Amish young woman raised her apron and wiped her eye.

Shedding a tear when he left? What had Clayton said to her? Lilly wondered.

Chapter 39

Apparently Tony had not said anything to Clay about a weekend in New York City because Clay didn't mention it when he brought Rebecca home. Perhaps it was because Tony knew Mr. Lockwood wouldn't be around for too long. To Lilly that meant Tony could show empathy for others. A desirable trait.

The idea of visiting New York was like a pesky gnat constantly buzzing around in her mind. Lilly had to talk to Laura.

Rebecca was doing laundry when Lilly told her she had to go to visit her sister in Berryville.

"Go ahead, Miss Lilly. I will make lunch for Josiah, and I will be here when Emily and Flossie come from school if you aren't back."

"Thank you. I hate to make that trip again, but I have to go."

Rebecca asked no questions and neither did Josiah when he saw Lilly hitch Jack to the buggy and drive down the lane. No one saw the concerned and puzzled look on his face as he watched from the field.

Lilly hurried Jack along. Questions whirled around in her head as she rode. Should she even mention what Tony Vello had proposed or let it drop? Was she being fair to her daughters? Was she being fair to Rebecca and Josiah for even considering the trip? The thought never surfaced that she might not be fair to Frank's memory. The idea could put too much guilt on her shoulders. Then she thought, as of yet she has done nothing wrong. Why should she be in such a jangle of nerves?

She drove into the lane that went by Clay's big house and over the rise farther down the lane to where the Richards's tenant house sat. She drove Jack to the front and tied the reins to a post. Laura was hoeing in the garden.

Lilly came around the side of the house. "Hello, Laura."

Laura looked up. "It must be mighty important for you to come unannounced. What's the matter?"

"Can we go inside? I don't want to take you away from your work but I've got to talk to you."

Laura leaned the hoe against a tree trunk. "You go on in and heat up the kettle while I wash up."

Lilly went ahead and put the filled kettle on the stove. She took two tea bags from the cupboard and put two mugs on the table. "Do you want to use that pretty teacup with the yellow flowers?"

"No. Addie bought me that. She thought I needed something to pretty up the place so I keep it just to look at it," Laura replied.

"I'm sure she meant for you to use it," said Lilly.

"These old pottery mugs are good enough for me."

They sat opposite at the kitchen table.

231

"What has brought you here in desperation?" asked Laura.

"I'm not desperate," Lilly defended herself. "I came to ask your advice."

The tea kettle started to whistle and Lilly got up to pour hot water into their mugs.

"Laura, did you meet Clayton's friend, Anthony Vello, when he was here taking care of Clayton's father?"

"I did. He has a certain air about him and he talks like a Yankee."

"The Civil War is over, Laura. He's rather nice. This is my dilemma and I need you to tell me what to do. He has asked me to come to New York City for a weekend. I can take the girls or Rebecca or all three of them."

Laura sipped her tea. "I guess you either want me to tell you to go or forget the question ever came up."

"Yes, I do. You are wiser than I am in many ways. It is a chance to get away and see what a city looks like. Frank would never go anywhere. I wouldn't want word to get out, but…"

"Why do you even question, Lilly? Go! If you don't you will always wonder if you should have. People talk no matter what. If I were in your shoes, I wouldn't give it a second thought. Have the time of your life because you may not get the chance again. The girls can stay here."

Lilly rose from her chair and hugged Laura around the neck. "I guess I needed your blessing. Tony said that he was going to suggest that Clayton and Rebecca come also. He said it would be good for all three of us after losing Frank and Mr. Lockwood."

Lilly went back to her chair and sipped her tepid tea.

Laura posed an important question, "How do you feel about Clay's friend?"

Lilly hesitated as she thought about what Laura had asked. "I don't know. I think he likes me, but he is kind of smooth. He said this is an opportunity to get to know him better."

Laura set her mug on the table. "Another reason you should go."

Lilly sighed. "Thanks, Laura. I do value your opinion. I feel much better and I'm glad I came. I will let you know what I decide. The girls would love to come and spend a couple of days here. I guess I'd better let you get back to your garden. I feel like a giddy schoolgirl."

Laura took her mug to the sink. "I would love to feel like that...just once."

Lilly went to the door and Laura put her straw hat back on her head and picked up her work gloves.

"You deserve some happiness, Lilly."

They walked out onto the porch. Lilly went to the buggy and Laura went in the direction of the garden.

"Bye, Laura."

"Bye, Lilly."

Lilly felt like a different person on the way back to Boyce. She would wait to hear from either Tony or Clayton. Maybe she wouldn't hear from either.

Chapter 40

Two weeks passed. The girls finished school for the summer. Rebecca liked tending the vegetable garden, which was fine with Lilly. Josiah had worked from dawn to dusk to get the land plowed and cultivated for winter crops. *Roseville* was looking good.

It was a Wednesday morning when Clay arrived in the Model T. Lilly was in the kitchen. Her heart began beating like a drum because she was sure she knew why he had come. Rebecca must have heard the car because she came hurrying from the garden. Lilly watched from the kitchen as Clay got out of the car, took Rebecca's hand and brought it to his lips. Rebecca led him into the kitchen.

"Hello, Mrs. Pierce," said the tall, brawny Clay as he removed his driving cap.

"Clayton, how good to see you."

"I trust I am not interrupting your day."

"I was cutting up some vegetables for this evening's supper. Come in and have a seat. Would you care for a cup of coffee? Rebecca and I were about to have one."

"I would." He took a seat at the kitchen table. Rebecca put cups and saucers on the table. Lilly poured the coffee. "What brings you here on this nice day?"

"Tony called me from New York. He wants the three of us to come up for a weekend. He said he asked you about it when he was here the last time."

Lilly stirred cream into her coffee. "He did."

"What are your thoughts?"

Lilly didn't blink an eye. "I'd like to go. Only if you and Rebecca are going."

Clay laughed. "We'll be your chaperones and you'll be ours."

Lilly was enthused. "What do you think, Clayton? Do you want to go?"

"It is up to Rebecca."

Rebecca was shy. "I have never been to a big city. I will have to ask Josiah."

"If we do go, when are you considering?" asked Lilly.

"The latest train for Washington is six-thirty Friday evening. We will return on the six-ten on Sunday evening."

"That doesn't give us much time to prepare," said Lilly.

"Shall I go find Josiah?" asked Clay.

"He will be in for lunch. The girls are supposed to be helping him. Why don't you and Rebecca take a walk? I'll fix a picnic lunch and we can eat out under the tree."

"I should help."

"No, Rebecca. Clayton is our guest. You can keep him company."

"I like the sound of that," said Clay. "Come on, Rebecca, we'll get out from under Mrs. Pierce's feet."

Lilly was pleased with her shifty manoeuver. The young people deserved time to themselves.

Josiah and the girls came to the house for lunch. Emily and Flossie spied Rebecca and Clay sitting on the bench under the tree and ran to see them.

"Mister Clay. What are you doing here?" asked Emily.

"I came to see if you girls are as pretty as you were," he teased.

"You can't take Rebecca back," said Flossie.

Clay laughed. "No, Rebecca will stay here."

Josiah came to where they sat. "You girls better get washed up. Your mother will have lunch for us."

He nodded to acknowledge Clay.

"I will go in and help Miss Lilly." Rebecca rose quickly and went to the house.

Clay stood up. "Josiah, I came to ask if Rebecca can go with Mrs. Pierce and me for the weekend. You met my army pal, Tony. He wants to show us the highlights of New York City."

"What does Miss Lilly want?"

"She wants to go."

"And, Rebecca?"

"She also wants to go if it is all right with you."

236

"Rebecca is old enough to make her own decisions. Miss Lilly needs to get away from this place to sort out her feelings."

"What do you mean by that?" asked Clay.

"When her husband died it threw her into a whole new way of life. She needs to be away from the girls and away from this farm to see in what direction her life is headed."

"I never thought of that. New York City would definitely be a change."

"It will be good for you, too."

"So you don't mind if Rebecca goes?"

"Women who have never been to a big city need to go. There is much that goes on that magazines don't tell them."

Josiah left to wash up for lunch.

Lilly and Rebecca brought the picnic lunch to the outdoor table where benches were placed on both sides. The talk was about how Emily and Flossie were a big help to Josiah, how Ef had learned to handle the sheep and the cows, whether it would be more profitable to give up the sheep and concentrate on meat cattle and how the horse man was impressed with the foal Lilly had sold to Clay. Nothing was said about a weekend in New York City.

Josiah, Emily and Flossie finished their milk and molasses cookies and the three headed back to the barn. Lilly wondered why they were anxious to help Josiah until she found out he promised to build them a tree house.

Lilly went back into the house and Rebecca stayed outside until Clay left. When he had gone, she brought in the tablecloth and jug of tea that were left on the table.

"Had Clayton talked to Josiah?" asked Lilly.

"Josiah says I am old enough to make my own decisions and he is not against it. Clay said he will phone when he gets home."

"Laura had offered that the girls can stay with her. I asked Clay to check with her."

"Does that mean we will go?"

"Yes, Rebecca. We will get the clothes ready we need to take and Friday evening we will be on our way. What do you think of that?"

That evening Rebecca took Emily and Flossie to read them a bedtime story. Josiah was sitting on the bench, smoking his pipe, enjoying the balmy evening.

Lilly went out to sit by him. "You are fine with Rebecca and me leaving over the weekend?"

"It is not for me to say."

"Do you think I am making a mistake?"

Josiah shifted his body to look at her. "We all make mistakes. The girls will be cared for and I will care for your farm. You have not had the luxury to get away from your responsibilities. If you go, Miss Lilly, you will never have to feel as though life cheated you."

She sat for a quiet moment. "Laura said almost the same thing. Do you think that is how she feels? Cheated?"

"I don't know. I do know that you need to have time away to think."

Lilly sighed. "You are right. Josiah would you mind calling me Lilly? I don't like to refer to you as hired help. You are Josiah Bly and a wiser man I have yet to meet."

"It would be my pleasure, Lilly." That crooked smile appeared. "Are you sure me calling you Lilly won't harm your status in the community?"

She waved the question away. "I am going to New York City and I hope to return with a new outlook on life."

"I'll be here," he said.

Chapter 41

Josiah hitched Jack to the buggy. Emily and Flossie each took a tote bag to carry their clothes. Lilly had a small suitcase and Rebecca carried Lilly's tapestried satchel. There was excited chatter as Josiah loaded the buggy. He would take the girls to Laura's then leave Lilly and Rebecca at Clay's.

Alex was there to drive Clay, Rebecca and Lilly to the Bluemont station in the Franklin. The car was crowded with the four of them and their baggage but no one seemed to mind.

Once they started, Alex said, "Addie said she would like to go along with you. I suggested we could go one day for a long overdue honeymoon."

"Did she want to go to New York for a honeymoon?" asked Lilly.

"She said she would rather go back to Leadville and stay in Caleb's run-down camp."

"What is he going to do with that?" asked Clay "From the way Lottie describes the place, it's not worth anything."

"It is the most peaceful place on earth," answered Alex. "It's high in the mountains with a clear rippling stream that rushes over rocks. You can sit on a boulder and let your mind drift away."

Alex shifted the car into low to pull the auto up the curvy road from Pine Grove.

"That sounds like where I should be headed," mused Lilly.

When they reached Bluemont, the train from Washington had delivered its passengers and was headed for the roundabout to go back east.

The three bound for New York City retrieved their luggage and walked to the platform. Alex turned the Franklin around and left. He would be back to pick them up on Sunday.

Clay ushered the women to a seat near the front of the railcar. Lilly and Rebecca sat side by side, Clay sat facing them.

"We'll change trains in Washington in Union Station," Clay informed. "There will be stops along the way. We won't reach New York until midnight or later."

"Won't everything be shut down?" asked Lilly.

Clay was confident. "They say New York is the city that never sleeps. I have been assured that the hotel knows we will be late arrivals."

"When will we eat?" inquired Lilly, who was beginning to lament she hadn't packed sandwiches or eaten more heartily before they left.

"There is a dining car on the train from Washington. It will be a late supper that should hold us until breakfast," said Clay.

Rebecca had been quiet.

"Lilly looked over at her as the train began its descent down the other side of the mountain. "What are your thoughts, Rebecca?"

"I think I will be happy to come back home," she replied.

**

The train from Washington arrived at Grand Central Terminal in New York City around 1:00 a.m. There were less stops on the evening train according to the conductor. There were more than enough to suit Lilly. Just when she started to doze off the whistle blew and the train slowed to a stop. Then with a jerk it started up again.

The fare in the dining car was enough to hold her until morning, but it also gave her dyspepsia. Maybe the irritation would go away.

Neither she nor Rebecca were prepared for the vastness of the train terminal that covered acres of land. Once they stepped out onto the platform, Clay motioned to a porter who loaded their luggage on an iron-wheeled cart. Lilly held onto Rebecca's arm and Rebecca gripped Clay's like a hawk carrying its prey.

"We'll walk to the front of the building and get a taxi," he said to the two apprehensive women.

It wasn't a short walk. The women gaped at the ornate interior of the huge building. There were many people milling around even at this early hour of the morning.

Clay tipped the porter with a dollar bill. Lilly and Rebecca's eyes widened at this extravagance.

"He had to haul that cart a long way," was Clay's explanation.

The porter hailed a yellow cab for them. Clay opened the back door for the ladies to get into the back seat. He sat up front with the driver, who had taken care of the luggage.

"59 West 44th Street," ordered Clay.

"The Algonquin," said the driver. "One of our city's finest."

It was a half-hour later when they entered the opulent lobby of the hotel. There were people sitting around in leather chairs in the lobby.

Clay came to where the women sat. A bell-hop carried keys and took their luggage, Rebecca's satchel tucked under his arm and a suitcase in each hand. They followed him to the elevator.

It was a shaky ride up to the fourth floor. The rooms they were given were across the hall from each other. The bell-hop twisted the key in the lock to the women's room, sat their two traveling bags inside and turned to open Clay's door.

"I'll knock on your door in the morning," said Clay.

"What time will that be," asked Lilly.

"Nine o'clock. We'll get some good sleep. We will have breakfast here at the hotel. Tony said he would meet us here."

At the sound of Tony's name a pang of uneasiness shot through Lilly. Should she have come?

She and Rebecca entered the room that was decorated with mahogany furniture. A high bed, chest of drawers, small desk, two leather chairs and a clothes closet.

"Oh, Miss Lilly. Have you ever seen anything so grand?" Then Rebecca opened a door and shouted aloud, "Oh my!"

Lilly hurried to see what had caused this response. Indoor plumbing! There was a sink, commode and bathtub and a steam radiator for warmth. Lilly wondered how much this place was costing Tony.

It was a balmy night and Lilly decided to open a window. With the sounds from the street and the street lights making it seem like day, she closed the window. This was like a whole new world.

Sleep wasn't easy to come for Lilly. She lay in bed next to Rebecca, who had gone to sleep almost as soon as her head hit the pillow.

Lilly had too much to think about. She didn't have to worry about her girls because they were safe at Laura's. She didn't have to worry about the farm because Josiah would care for it.

Money was still a worry, but she had managed so far. How to keep the farm viable was a constant sub-conscious needling. She thought of the changes in her life in the past nine months: Frank's death, the sole responsibility of her daughters, the arrival of Josiah and then Rebecca, the lonely feeling that crept in when she least expected it. Foremost in her mind was her biggest worry, Tony. Lilly wasn't sure how she felt about him.

Chapter 42

At nine o'clock sharp, Clay knocked on the door of the women's room. They were dressed for the day. Rebecca wore her long hair in a braid and wound it in a bun. She wore a plain yellow cotton dress and a straw hat. Lilly carried a parasol of beige organdy. She wore a soft, shapeless dress of French blue with a beige straw hat decorated with a band of colorful dried flowers.

"A lovely pair," acknowledged Clay when they stepped out into the hall.

"A shaky pair,' said Lilly. "I guess we are ready to meet the day."

When they reached the lobby, Tony rose from the leather chair he was sitting in and came to greet them. Dashing is the only way to describe his dress and manner. He wore a summer-weight tan suit with a fitted jacket and pinched waist, white shirt, and brown and tan wingtip shoes. His smile was wide and welcoming.

He shook Clay's hand and acknowledged Rebecca. After taking's Lilly's hand he leaned forward and brushed his cheek against hers. Lilly was glad Clay and Rebecca were gazing around the lobby and didn't notice. She hoped they didn't.

"I have been waiting all week," Tony said. "Let's go into the Pergola Room for breakfast and then we'll tire ourselves out seeing the sights. What do you say?"

Clay spoke for the three. "We're all for it."

Lilly was glad Clay answered. She was still ruffled from the feeling of Tony's smooth cheek against hers.

In the large dining room they sat at a table for four. A waiter came and took their orders. He returned with coffee for all four before the meal.

Tony was in his element. "This hotel is a favorite of writers and stage people," he informed. "The lineup for today is going to be a stop at Woolworth's, a carriage ride through Central Park, dinner at Delmonico's, and, if we are up to it, a play on Broadway."

"I'm tired all ready," remarked Lilly. "I hope I sleep better tonight."

"I slept well," said Rebecca.

"It's not always easy to sleep in a different bed," Tony said. "Clay and I had to sleep in barn lofts when we were in the service and then on narrow cots in tents. We could probably sleep on a pile of tin if we had to."

Clay laughed. "I probably could. You got that cushy job as an orderly in the hospital."

"Field hospital," reminded Tony.

Lilly stirred cream into her coffee. "Josiah said he met Andrew Caldwell in a hospital. That's how he got to Virginia."

Rebecca was surprised. "I didn't know that."

"Yes, his Amish German came in handy. He was sent to guard an injured German officer and Andrew was recovering from a leg wound."

"I'll bet none of his buddies knew he was German," surmised Tony.

Lilly looked over at him with a sharp look. "What difference would that make? You are Italian but you and Josiah are both Americans."

It was Tony's turn to be surprised.

"It looks like you ordered pleasant weather for us," said Clay, as a way of softening Lilly's remark.

Tony nodded, still feeling the sting. "You picked a perfect weekend to come."

The waiter brought their plates loaded with breakfast foods.

Lilly was uneasy. Why did she feel she had to defend Josiah? She should apologize, but not now. Perhaps the food would sweeten her disposition.

"Tell us about Woolworth's, Tony." Lilly suggested.

He came to life. "It is the tallest building in the world at 60 stories. It houses the F. W. Woolworth headquarters."

"I've read about those stores," Lilly said.

"F. W. Woolworth 5&10's. The building is at 233 Broadway across from City Hall. Once we get this breakfast down we can walk there."

Lilly felt better.

They left the Algonquin with Rebecca holding onto Clay's arm and Lilly holding onto Tony's. The sidewalks were uneven and Lilly had a low heel so she deemed it wise to have ballast in case she tripped.

Tony led the way.

"Tony, I need to apologize for sounding so short with you at breakfast. I'm not sure what came over me."

He placed his other hand atop hers as she held onto his arm. "I deserved it. Let's just enjoy the day ahead." He looked down at her and flashed his dazzling smile.

She squeezed his arm. "Thank you."

They passed many small shops along the way until they saw the spiked tower of the Woolworth building.

"It reaches into the sky," marveled Rebecca.

"It beats anything in Washington, D.C." was Clay's response.

Lilly stood open-mouthed.

"Wait until you walk into the lobby," said Tony.

They crossed the street after waiting for cars and cabs and horse-drawn wagons.

"You certainly have a lot of traffic up here," Lilly observed.

"People have more money after the war ended. The city is growing fast. Bringing in people from all over the country and the world."

"I don't think that is the case in the farming communities."

Tony looked at her as they neared the building. "You work too hard. Lovely lady that you are, you should have an easier life."

Lilly smiled up at him. "Tony, your words make me feel like a queen."

"You are in my sight," he replied.

A doorman opened the door and the four-some stepped into the lobby. The three visitors were in awe. There was a vaulted ceiling with stained glass lighting, mosaics, and murals on every balcony as their eyes adjusted to the grandeur.

"We'll take the elevator to the 5th floor where they have an observation deck. They crossed the smooth as glass floor and Lilly grabbed Tony's arm again. The elevator door opened. They stood at the back as people crowded in. The elevator stopped at each floor for riders to get on or off until the operator announced the 5th.

They wound their way through the people in front of them. Rebecca took a deep breath. "I thought I would suffocate."

Clay took her hand. "We were packed in like sardines."

She chuckled.

They stepped out onto the observation deck far above the city. Clay and Rebecca walked to the rail and looked down.

"The people look like ants," observed Rebecca. "Busy, busy."

Clay laughed. "Everyone in a hurry to go nowhere."

Tony suggested, "Lilly, you will get a great view if you go to the railing."

Lilly stood a couple of feet inside the door. "This is close enough for me. My legs feel like rubber."

"I'll hold onto you," he encouraged.

"Thanks, but I'm satisfied."

Rebecca stepped up onto the concrete holding the post to get a wider view and Lilly felt like she would swoon.

"Rebecca, step back off there before you fall!"

Clay laughed aloud. "There are windows all around. There is no way she could fall."

"Lilly and I will step back in. There are chairs for visitors. We'll take it easy until you two are ready," said Tony.

Lilly was more than glad to step back inside. "I don't even like to go up on a stepladder," she confessed.

Tony led her to where two chairs sat side by side. "I didn't know you were afraid of heights or I wouldn't have suggested coming here."

She touched his hand. "Don't feel it was a mistake. I'm happy we came. This is a beautiful place. The likes I'll never see again."

He took her hand. "But you will. I want you to bring the girls."

She looked at him. "Tony, you know I can't afford this. I came because Clay and Rebecca needed to get away. They have much to think about."

"You didn't want to see me?"

Tony was hard to resist. "If I'm honest I have to say that, yes, I wanted to see you again."

He kissed the hand he held. "That makes me feel better."

Lilly removed her hand from his. There were people coming off the elevator.

"My husband has only been dead for nine months."

"What difference does that make?"

Lilly rolled her eyes and wagged her head. "Oh, Tony. You and I are from two different worlds."

The door to the observation deck opened and out came Clay and Rebecca. They both wore wide smiles.

Rebecca said if she was a bird she would fly around and watch all the people staring out."Don't you think the birds would wonder about us as much as we wonder about them, especially the pigeons?" she said.

"I never thought of that," said Tony.

"I don't think any of us did," said Clay.

Tony hailed a cab when they left the Woolworth building and they rode to Central Park. There they climbed into a fancy carriage driven by a driver in a black suit and top hat. It was like being back in the country with the trees and flowers but there were lovely walks and benches and ponds of water. One could live in the city and feel they were in the country.

When they were through Tony suggested a cold lemonade. They sat outside a small shop relishing their drink and watched the vast array of people who made up this city. What bothered Lilly the most were the panhandlers. They seemed to be on every street.

They spent the rest of the afternoon going in and out of the many shops. Lilly thought there was

251

a shop for everything: bread shop, bakery shop, meat shop, sandwich shop, wine shop. The list was endless. It was obvious the people didn't grow their own food. Where would they grow it?

In one of the shops she bought fancy hair ribbons for Emily and Flossie. Then they went into a candy store where she bought them lollipops and a tin of fudge. She bought Josiah peppermint sticks. They had been his favorites at Christmas, she remembered

It was almost six o'clock when Tony hailed a taxi to take them to Delmonico's for dinner. Tony had reserved a table so they didn't have to wait in the line that was forming.

"Saturday night is always crowded," he said.

After they were seated he ordered a bottle of red wine with four glasses.

"Tony, I don't think Rebecca and I should drink wine."

"It will help you relax and it goes great with the steak."

A tough-looking man, nattily dressed, came by and stopped at the table. "Hey, Tony. Where you been hidin'?" He wore a gold watch and diamond stick-pin in his tie.

Tony stood up. "Spending time at Belmont."

Clay wondered if this was one of the men Tony had trouble with because Tony seemed to be on alert.

The pock-faced man looked over at Lilly and gave her an appreciative once over, which made her uncomfortable. She did not like this rude man.

"Ain't you gonna' introduce me to your lady friend, Tony?"

She looked the man squarely in the eye. "My name is Mrs. Lilly Pierce. Is that introduction enough?"

He raised both his large hands. "Whoa. She's all yours, Tony. See you around."

"Who is that dreadful man?" asked Lilly.

"One of the biggest gangsters in the city."

She gulped. "Maybe I will have a sip of wine."

By the time they finished dinner, the city was beginning to come alive. Lilly and Rebecca were ready to go back to the Algonquin.

Tony wasn't ready to call it a night. "There's a vaudeville act not far from here. We could take that in and you'll still be in bed by ten."

It wouldn't be right not to honor the host so Lilly agreed. On their way, they passed a café where a lot of different men were hanging around a man sitting at a table in the window

The four of them stopped

Lilly spied a derby hat and a cane on the table. Gray eyes, cold as steel, glanced up at them sending a shiver through Lilly.

Tony waved, the man smiled in recognition and nodded. Tony hurried them on. The theatre was another block away.

"He must be important," said Clay.

"That's 'Bat' Masterson. He writes a sports column for the *Morning Telegraph*. You've probably heard of him. He was a sheriff and gunfighter in his younger days in the West."

Clay laughed. "Too bad Addie isn't here. She loves all those western stories. He could probably tell quite a few."

"He loves boxing. I met him around the arenas. I'll bet he was something in his day. Although he's over fifty now, the young toughs all quiet down when he walks in."

They went to the vaudeville act that was filled with music and comedy acts before they returned to the Algonquin for the night. Clay and Rebecca walked toward the elevator while Lilly said goodnight to Tony.

"What time does your train leave?" he asked.

"Clay said 12:15."

"That will give us time for a long breakfast."

"Tony, thank you for such a pleasurable day. I am glad I came."

He took her hand. "I am too."

Then he pulled her to him and kissed her.

She wasn't prepared for the tantalizing thrill of his lips on hers. She hadn't been kissed in a long time.

"A perfect ending to a perfect day," he said and smiled broadly. "Do you want me to accompany you to your room?"

"No, Rebecca and Clay will be at the elevator. "I hope they didn't see your forward move."

"Clay knows how I feel about you."

"Tony, I've noticed the women here. They are your style. I am thirty-one and a widow with two children. This is your world, mine is back in Virginia."

"I'm thirty, never been married, and you are hard to dislodge. We're still on for breakfast?"

Lilly couldn't help but smile. "We're still on for breakfast."

Chapter 43

The 6:10 was only ten minutes late when it rolled into the Bluemont station. Alex was waiting for them.

"You three look like you've had a successful weekend."

"I think you can say we did New York. At least, it feels like we did. We three slept most of the way back, as much sleep as you can get on a train," informed Clay.

"Addie said you ladies should stay at Clay's place overnight and go home tomorrow."

"I told Josiah we would be home this evening," said Lilly.

Alex persisted. "Laura won't mind if the girls stay tonight. The road to Boyce is dark and curvy. It is wise to remain at Clay's house."

"Alex is right," said Clay.

Lilly looked out the window of the auto and saw the dark setting in. The road down the mountain into Pine Grove was dangerous during the daytime and more dangerous at night. "I know you are both right. I'll check in with Laura when we reach your place, Clayton."

Rebecca didn't seem to mind the idea of spending the night at Clay's. She was smiling at him.

Emily and Flossie were already in bed when they reached the Richards's house.

"They had a long day and they were tired," explained Laura.

Lilly hugged her sister. "It's best that I don't wake them. We'll come by and pick them up around nine. Is that all right with you?"

"That's good. How was your trip?"

"Laura, I'm glad I went. One day I will have to tell you all about it. I believe Clayton, Rebecca and I are ready for a good night's sleep."

Lilly got back into the car where the others were waiting. "Laura is fine with us picking them up in the morning. Alex are you driving back to *Lockwood* tonight?"

"Yes. My Franklin has good headlamps."

Clay said, "Be sure and tell Addie that we saw 'Bat' Masterson. She won't sleep a wink."

"Does she still read those western books?" asked Lilly.

"Every one she can get her hands on," answered Alex.

He parked the Franklin at the back of Clay's house where they unloaded the sparse luggage they had taken.

Alex idled the car. "It's good you are back. Don't be surprised if you get an invitation from Addie to come for a meal. Addie will want to hear every detail. She is always curious about what is over the next hill."

"I could use one of Ella's meals," said Clay. "So she had better invite me."

Alex laughed. "That will give us the man's point of view as well as the ladies'."

Faith was nowhere to be seen when Clay, Rebecca and Lilly came into the kitchen. There was a warm pot of potato soup on the stove and sandwiches wrapped in wax paper on the table.

"Faith never lets me down," said Clay. "Rebecca your room is ready and Mrs. Pierce can use the room adjoining."

Lilly was grateful. "Thank you, Clayton. Once we put our traveling bags away we can have some of that soup. I, for one, plan to sleep like a log."

Rebecca chuckled. "It will be nice to hear the sounds of summer and not the rattle of cars all night long."

"Or see the lights that never shut down," added Clay.

"It was a memorable two days." Lilly enjoined. She picked up her suitcase and headed for the room she would use.

Rebecca followed close behind.

Faith had left towels, face cloths and ewers of water on the dry sinks. She must have guessed the women would be spending the night.

The two women felt refreshed when they went to the kitchen to put bowls and plates on the table. Clay came in with combed hair and freshly scrubbed face and hands.

"It is good to be home, isn't it?" he said.

Lilly sighed. "I will be glad to have my girls with me. I have never been away from them for this long. What about you, Rebecca? Will you be glad to get back to *Roseville?*"

Rebecca didn't answer Lilly right away. She was honest. "I am at home both here and at *Roseville.*"

Lilly didn't say anything.

The three ate their sandwiches and soup. Lilly made an excuse to retire and left Clay and Rebecca alone. She had seen enough silent language exchanged between the two to know Rebecca had developed a caring for Clay. She thought he felt the same. Or was it an infatuation on Clay's part because Rebecca had taken care of his father? Rebecca had been Clay's strength to help him through that ordeal.

Rebecca was young and might be hurt. That possibility weighed on Lilly's mind. Was it her place to warn Rebecca before she cared too much? Lilly changed into her nightgown, drained of energy. She had enough worries. Rebecca was Josiah's problem. That was the answer. Lilly would talk with him.

Chapter 44

Clay, Rebecca and Lilly were eating breakfast the next morning when a familiar sound reached Lilly's ears. "That's Jack pulling my buggy!"

Before Clay could leave his seat there was a soft knock on the kitchen door. Faith answered it.

Clay went to the door. "Josiah! I am surprised to see you here."

"When my four ladies didn't return last night, I figured they were spending the night here."

"You figured right," agreed Clay. He shook Josiah's hand. "Come in and have coffee with us. We're finishing up our breakfast. Emily and Flossie are still at their aunt's house."

They went into the dining rom. Rebecca was out of her chair and ran to meet her brother with a warm hug.

Lilly wanted to do the same. She smiled. "I heard Jack and the buggy. It's nice to see you, Josiah."

His clear blue eyes settled on hers. "I thought I would save Clay the time of driving you home."

His face was tanned, muscles well-defined under a blue work shirt with the sleeves rolled up to the elbow. The sun had bleached his blonde hair to a sparkling sheen. He stood a few inches shorter than Clay with a pleasurable smile that gave Lilly a warm feeling. Her farm helper looked right nice.

Lilly drew her eyes away. "Have you eaten breakfast?"

"Early on. I could use a hot cup of coffee."

Faith was already on her way with an extra mug and a pot of coffee. She filled their cups. Back to the kitchen she shuffled and returned with a plate of eggs and bacon and a fresh baked biscuit. She placed the plate in front of Josiah. "Looks like you could use some fattenin' up."

Clay let out a belly laugh. "It's good you don't live here or she'd have you looking like me."

Faith turned with a "Humph."

Rebecca was quick to say, "You are not fat. You are like me. We are tall and strong."

Clay looked over at her with a benevolent smile.

"That's a fact," said Josiah. "And this food hits the spot."

"I told Laura we would get the girls around nine. How does the weather look, Josiah?" asked Lilly.

"It should be clear until we get home. There are some storm clouds building up to the south."

"Then the sooner we get started, the better. Are you packed Rebecca?"

"I am, Miss Lilly."

Josiah finished his coffee while the two women went for their traveling bags.

"How was your trip?" Josiah asked Clay.

"Eye opening," was his response.

Josiah took both bags. The four went to the buggy and he put them behind the back seat.

Clay and Rebecca held back a bit, but not before Clay took Rebecca's hand and said, "I will be down to see you."

Lilly climbed up onto the front seat. She was eager to get Emily and Flossie and be on their way to Boyce.

The two girls came running out of the house as the buggy came down the lane.

Lilly was off the seat in a flash and drew her precious girls close. "I have missed you two," she said, and kissed each on the cheek. "Did you behave for Aunt Laura?"

"We were good, weren't we Aunt Laura?" hollered Emily.

Laura was on the porch holding their tote bags. "Good as gold."

The girls ran to give her a hug and pick up their bags before they climbed into the buggy and took a seat on each side of Rebecca. She put her arms around them.

"Did you like New York City?" Flossie asked Rebecca.

"I did, but I am happy to be back home."

"We're happy to have you and Momma back," confided Emily. "I hope you don't go away like that again."

Lilly smiled to herself. She had left the city with mixed emotions. Most of her doubts were about Anthony Vello.

The big white farm house was a welcoming sight when Josiah turned the horse into the drive. His voice was low. "You've been quiet," he said to Lilly. "Did the big city leave you with questions?"

Her voice was above a whisper. "When we have time by ourselves I'll tell you about it. I have other concerns on my mind."

"I sold a ram and six sheep for a good price the other day. They were ones you can do without. Maybe that news will help lighten your burdens."

Lilly turned and smiled at him. "That will help with one worry, but not with the uncertainties running around in my head."

"Lilly, life is too short to wear yourself down with things you have no control over."

She breathed a heavy sigh. He was right. But, sometimes a person can't help worrying.

Chapter 45

It was Friday before Lilly found time alone with Josiah. Emily and Flossie were invited to a birthday party. Rebecca offered to take Jack and the buggy to drive them over and bring them home. She wanted to look at material and patterns at the department store in Boyce while the girls were at the party.

Josiah was working near the barn. Lilly took a jug of lemonade and asked him to come sit on the bench under the oak tree.

He went to the well, soaked his handkerchief in cold water, and wiped his face before he washed his hands. He came to where she sat with a warm smile. Lilly poured cold lemonade for each of them.

"I have been wondering what puts a pinched look on your usual pleasant countenance."

"I hoped you didn't notice. Josiah, I am concerned about what I have seen pass between Rebecca and Clayton. I don't want her getting hurt. They have much different backgrounds."

Josiah took a drink of his lemonade. "Is it Rebecca you are worrying about or is it yourself?"

She became indignant. "I don't know what you mean."

"You are confused about Clay's friend. I'm sure he showed you a good time in New York.

Rebecca and Clay have to work things out for themselves."

"Don't you care if your sister has a broken heart?"

"Of course I care. Women don't die of broken hearts, especially if they are young. Don't be too quick to write Clay off. He has a lot of substance."

Lilly let a sigh escape. "I'm not sorry I brought it up. I suppose you are right. It is none of my business, but I would hate to see Rebecca unhappy."

"You haven't told me how you feel about Clay's friend."

Lilly was pensive. "I don't know how I feel. He is not like any man I've met. He says the same about me."

"You are different. You are kind and caring and you make a man feel as though he is worth something."

Those words made her head snap up. "Josiah you are worth more than I can say. I don't know where I would be now if you hadn't come here."

A sly smile with the raise of an eyebrow appeared. "See what I mean? Men like to feel appreciated."

"When I left New York, I made it clear that my home is here in Virginia and his is in the big city."

"And I'm sure he accepted that."

She stuttered "Well, I…I…I don't know."

Josiah leaned back against the trunk of the tree. "You will see him again. He is not the kind of man who gives up easy. Meanwhile, Clay and Rebecca will know their hearts and you will have to sort out yours."

Josiah sat for a long moment before he leaned forward and rose to his feet. "I need to get back to my work. Thank you for the lemonade." He looked straight into her eyes. "The man in New York City is not the only man who cares for you," he said. Josiah Bly turned and walked off toward the barn.

Lilly sat and watched him leave. *What is wrong with me? I have no right to let other men cloud my brain when Frank has only been gone for 10 months.*

This conversation with Josiah wasn't what she had expected. She felt more mixed up than before. She vowed to keep her own counsel regarding Rebecca.

What about Anthony Vello? He held no secret that he was fond of her. He was dashing and fun and he appeared to have plenty of money. Where it came from she wasn't sure. The time in the city was like a fantasy. She admitted to herself that she hadn't thought of the farm or any responsibilities connected with it. It was a weekend of gay abandon and one she might like to experience again.

Lilly shook her head and came back to the present. She was sitting under the oak tree in her back yard enjoying a glass of lemonade. Her daughters would return from a birthday party with excited chatter about their day, and Rebecca would be enthused about the new pattern and material she had bought. Josiah would come for supper and retire to his room above the porch. This was Lilly's life. Was it enough?

**

Clay telephoned on Saturday. There would be a horse show on Sunday in Berryville. Would Lilly, Rebecca and the girls like to go? Lilly didn't need to ask, but she did.

"Clayton, thank you for the invitation. Rebecca and the girls are delighted. I have much to do to catch up on bookwork so I will stay here. What time will you be by?"

"Eleven."

"Would you like to have me prepare a picnic basket?"

"No thank you, Mrs. Pierce. It will be my treat." That was fine with Lilly.

"Then we shall see you in the morning. Good-bye, Clayton."

"Bye, Mrs. Pierce."

There was catch-up work to do in the office, which meant Lilly had not told a fib. The day would give Clay and Rebecca time to be alone with the girls for insurance to quell any rumors.

It also meant that Lilly and Josiah would have to work together to map out lineage charts. Addie had taught both of them how to follow the blood line of the horses and the sheep with what information Frank had left. Addie had already made out the charts for the cows Alex had sold to Lilly.

Maybe Lilly would get the hang of it, but it wasn't her favorite task.

Chapter 46

Clay Lockwood arrived at eleven. He looked bright and rested. He wore a short-sleeved white shirt, tan trousers and a plaid summer driving cap.

Rebecca had worked into the early hours of the morning sewing a dress. A long chestnut braid was wound into a bun that sat under a fashionable straw hat Lilly had lent to her. The dress she had made was plain with a dropped waist and a hem below the knee. In New York Lilly noticed waists were dropping and hems were shortening. Apparently Rebecca had noticed the same. The dress was Nile green, summer-weight cotton with white lace collar and cuffs.

Lilly saw the look of admiration on Clay's face when Rebecca appeared.

Emily and Flossie were dressed in their Sunday best with white cotton stockings and Mary Jane shoes. They wore the hair ribbons their mother bought in New York. Lilly couldn't help but feel proud when the three walked to the Model T with Clay.

"When should we expect you back?" she called to Clay.

"Around five-thirty. No need to make supper. We'll eat at the Battletown in Berryville."

Lilly waved as the auto puttered down the drive. She saw Ef running around near the barn and knew Josiah must be out there. The bookwork was waiting so she might as well go and tell him she would need his help. Since that day they shared conversation and lemonade under the oak, when he as much as said he cared for her, they had not been together without Rebecca and her daughters present. Lilly wasn't sure how she would feel if it was just the two of them. She didn't want to go and ask him to come to the house. Bite the bullet, isn't that what people say?

Lilly strolled down to where she saw Josiah resting on a pile of straw twirling a piece between his fingers. His straw hat shaded his face.

"I saw Ef running around and thought you were working down here."

He looked up and pushed his hat back. "I'm working my brain," he replied.

"What about?"

"Lots of things."

"Rebecca and the girls are gone for the day. I thought it would be good to get caught up on these animal charts we are supposed to be doing. I will need your help."

He threw down the piece of straw he had been twirling and sat up. "Lilly, do you have plans for the direction this farm is going?"

He got to his feet and came to stand beside her.

She stepped away to face him. "I don't know what you mean. I suppose it will go as it has always gone, once I pay off that debt Frank left me with."

"Don't sound bitter. I'm sure it wasn't your husband's idea to depart this life."

They turned and started walking toward the house. "I'm sorry if I sounded that way. This place is just one big worry for me from the time I get up in the morning until I fall asleep at night."

"I have been thinking. I have some ideas. I'm still your hired man so stop me if you need to, but I would like to tell you about them."

"Josiah, I have told you that you are more than a hired man. I value your opinion. God knows, I need someone to help me sort out this mess. Let's work on this animal history and then you can tell me about them."

They walked into the kitchen. Ef followed them in and went to a corner where a light breeze was wafting through.

"Do you want some cold tea?" asked Lilly.

"I would. It's a hot one out there today."

They took their glasses of tea to the office area where Lilly had papers strewn on a table. "We have started on the charts for the horses. Do you want to finish those?"

"Might as well," said Josiah. He took a seat at the table.

Lilly put Frank's notes together and began to sift through them. "I'll pull out only the horse information and you can record." Lilly didn't trust her handwriting. She felt shaky with just her and Josiah in close quarters.

Lilly sounded as lighthearted as she was able. "Clayton said he was treating the girls and Rebecca to dinner at the Battletown Inn in Berryville. If it is all right with you, I thought we could have toasted ham and cheese sandwiches with deviled eggs, and sliced tomatoes."

He looked up with clear blue eyes she always found refreshing. "Why not have cold ham and cheese sandwiches. It's almost too hot to eat."

Fine with Lilly. "That's even better. The eggs are made and the tomatoes sliced."

"What time is Clay bringing them back?"

"Five-thirty."

"Good. I think we can finish and then we can talk about what I have in mind that will help take some of the worry away from you."

Lilly sorted out the sheep information before she lugged the heavy file folder to the table from the desk. It was a two-piece heavy hardboard with two metal posts. She unscrewed the nuts and lifted the top hard board off. The cow charts were slipped over the posts with a paper separator waiting for other information to be laid on top of them.

"Do you think it matters if I file the sheep, then the horses, then the cattle?"

Josiah was working diligently. "I don't see what difference that would make. As long as you know where to find the information. That's what's important."

"I don't know how Frank knew where to find his information," said Lilly. "His notes were helter-skelter."

"You were fortunate to have Addie's help," said Josiah. "Here are the horse papers all up to date."

Lilly put the sheep papers in front of him. "That was faster than I expected. Here is the sheep data. This isn't going to be as easy."

"How do you know tracing the horse lineage was easy? Maybe I made it look that way."

Lilly chuckled. "Half of it was done and you only had to trace the three foals."

There were two holes in the long pieces of paper that she placed over the posts. She sat back and watched Josiah record information about the sheep. His printing was neat. Once he finished with Frank's notes he placed them in a tidy pile to be thrown away.

"Aren't you going to need those," asked Lilly.

"They are recorded. No sense in keeping clutter around."

That was true. The animal charts were all placed in one neat ledger causing the room to look more like an office instead of a hodge-podge of stacked papers.

Josiah looked at his pocket watch when they finished. "Three-thirty. Do you want to go outdoors and sit while I tell you about my ideas?"

"Let me refill our tea glasses and I'll meet you out on the bench."

Josiah stood and stretched. "It's a lazy day for me, Lilly."

"It's good for you once in a while. I enjoy the quiet, but I don't like too much of it. New York was never quiet."

"Do you think you will go back again?"

"I don't know." She picked up the empty glasses and went out of the room. She didn't see the disappointment on Josiah's face.

Lilly brought the tea to where he sat on the bench. A soft breeze had started and brought some relief to the hot day.

"Tell me what you have been thinking," she encouraged.

"I think you need to get rid of the sheep and raise cattle."

"But, it's the sale of wool and sheep that brings in money."

"Maybe it was profitable when your husband owned the wool business. It hasn't been this year," he advised. "The stock yards are right across the road. You have good access to the railroad for shipping. Also, to bring in good stock."

"I can't afford cows like Alex is raising," she countered.

He shifted on the bench to face her. "You don't have to. You can build them up as you go. Other cattle are less expensive. There is a big market for good beef. You can buy stock in the spring and sell it in the fall. That way you won't have to feed all winter. It will allow you to use some of the crop land for other uses."

"Isn't it risky?"

"Not as risky as sheep."

Lilly sat and thought for a long moment. What he said made sense. "How do you propose I get started? It is already the end of July."

"This is something to look at for next spring. If you can buy a couple of bred cows this fall, you will have a start along with the cows you bought from Alex. In the spring you can sell the sheep after the lambing and shearing. That will give you some leverage to increase cattle."

Lilly was to the point, "Josiah, I don't have the money to buy any more animals right now."

He didn't push. He made a suggestion, "You have three nice foals in the barn."

"I'll think about it," she said. Lilly took the empty tea glasses to the house. She took ham out of the ice box and sliced some pieces for sandwiches. It was nearly five o'clock. She and Josiah could eat before the girls returned at five-thirty. After she made the sandwiches and put the eggs and tomatoes on the table, she called out to Josiah to come in and eat.

He washed his face and hands at the well before he entered the kitchen. "I don't believe we've had the pleasure of just the two of us eating together since I came here," he noted.

Lilly smiled at him. "It won't be long before the quiet is broken. It is pleasant to sit and take our time."

He pulled the chair from the table for her to sit and took his seat next to her. "It isn't often I get the pleasure of your company by myself."

While they ate their supper, Lilly told him about the trip to New York. About the luxuries in the hotel, the ride through Central Park in the elaborate carriage, dinner at Delmonico's and the vaudeville show they had seen.

"It was good for Rebecca to get a taste of the city life," was all he said.

Lilly looked at the clock. "My goodness. It's quarter to six. Where do you suppose Clayton and the girls are?"

"I'm sure he'll be along."

Lilly cleared the table and washed the few dishes they had used. By six o'clock she was worried. At six-fifteen Josiah hitched Jack to the buggy and they left on the road to Berryville.

Chapter 47

They rode to Old Chapel before they saw the Model T leaning to one side. Emily and Flossie were crying when they came running to the buggy.

Emily's voice was high-pitched. "Momma, the wheel came off and when Clay tried to fix it the jack flew back and broke his leg. He looks awful, Momma."

Josiah and Lilly hurried to where Clay lay on the grass. Rebecca had thrown a shawl over him. His face was pale and contorted with pain.

Rebecca was kneeling beside Clay and rose from her knees. She burst into tears. "I didn't know what to do. I couldn't leave Clay and I couldn't send the girls by themselves."

"Of course you couldn't," said Lilly. She put her arm around Rebecca's shoulders.

"When did this happen?" asked Josiah as he pulled the shawl away and looked at Clay's injured leg.

"Within the last half-hour," Rebecca answered between sniffles. "I hoped someone would come along. What are we going to do, Josiah?"

"Lilly bring a blanket from the buggy and the jug of water."

She did as he asked. Her hands were shaking when she handed the jug to Josiah.

"You and Rebecca spread the blanket over him."

Clay was awake but weak.

Josiah wet his handkerchief with water and washed Clay's face. "Take a drink," he ordered. "We've got to get you back to Berryville to the doctor."

"I'm so sorry this happened," Clay said in a barely audible voice.

"Not your fault. You've got a bad break of your leg. I can try to stabilize it with a couple of small boards that are under the seat of the buggy. I don't know how we are going to get you up into the seat."

Emily and Flossie had stopped crying and Rebecca stood with a worried look. Josiah had Lilly drive the buggy as close to Clay as she dared.

He took out the boards, two-feet long, and tore his neckerchief into shreds. They weren't long enough. He tied them together. He told Lilly to get Emily's petticoat. With a pocket knife he sliced strips that he needed.

Clay did his best not to cry out in pain but he couldn't help it when Josiah slipped the ties under his leg and tied them around the boards which sat on either side of Clay's bloody, bone-exposed leg.

Emily and Flossie cried once again. With Rebecca under one arm, Josiah under the other and Lilly at his back they were able to get Clay onto his stable leg. He reached and held onto the iron rail of the front seat.

"Clay, I'll lift you from behind. Lilly you hold onto the splinted leg. Rebecca get into the buggy put your arm around his back and your shoulder under his armpit. On three we'll see if we can lift him to the seat."

"One, two, three!" Clay let out a shriek of pain but he was laying across the front seat.

Lilly threw the blanket over him and placed a rolled shawl between his legs. It was the best they could do.

Josiah ordered, "You four squeeze into the back seat and I'll ride Jack."

By the time they reached the Hawthorne house Clay had passed out. Dr. Hawthorne wasn't there but Dr. Burke was in finishing up some paperwork. Lilly pounded on the front door.

He came down the steps. One look at Clay and he didn't waste time. He ran back into the building and brought a folding stretcher. With Josiah and Lilly at one end and Rebecca and Dr. Burke at the other they were able roll Clay onto it. They carried him up the outside steps and up the front steps inside the building to the first floor.

"Second door on the left," said Dr. Burke. On a bed in the room the front spread and sheet were turned half-way down. He reached with one hand and pulled it the rest of the way. They rolled Clay onto the bed.

Dr. Burke pulled a syringe and vial from an enamel table drawer, filled the syringe and plunged it into Clay's arm.

279

"That's to bring him around," he explained.

Lilly told the girls to sit in chairs in the waiting room until she came for them.

After the injection, the physician put a leather cuff around Clay's arm to check his blood pressure. "It's not too bad," he said. He had pulled the blanket off from the injured leg. "When did this happen?"

"An hour or more ago," informed Josiah. "Apparently the wheel came off his car and when he tried to fix it the jack flew out from under the axle."

Dr. Hawthorne had come in the back door and heard the commotion. "Just got back from a house call. That's a nasty looking leg."

"We should take him to the hospital in Winchester," suggested Dr. Burke.

Dr. Hawthorne shook his head. "I'm not sure he could stand the trip. You've had plenty of experience with this kind of thing during the war. It's a clean break. Do you think, between the two of us, we could reduce the fracture?"

The two physicians mulled over the possibilities while three anxious onlookers wondered what they were considering.

"Who's the least shaky of you three?" asked Dr. Hawthorne.

"That would be Josiah," said Lilly without hesitation.

"Good. You ladies go into the waiting room. Josiah, we're going to teach you how to administer a bit of ether because he'll never be able to stand this without sedation."

Josiah opened his eyes wide. Lilly and Rebecca went to join the girls.

It was almost an hour later when Josiah came to meet them.

He wore a wide grin. "Maybe I'll go into medicine," he said. "Clay is sleeping like a baby. The doctors say his blood pressure and pulse are good and if infection doesn't set in, he'll be back on his feet in about six weeks."

Rebecca burst into tears causing Emily and Flossie to do the same.

"Tears of happiness, I trust," said Josiah.

"Thank God," said Lilly. "We need to call Alex and go down to let John and Laura know."

Dr. Burke came out to the waiting room. "Could one of you stay the night with him?"

Rebecca jumped up. "I will."

"He's going to be groggy until the sedation wears off but he's stable. If someone is with him it will give Dr. Hawthorne and me time to rest. Dr. Hawthorne will be upstairs and there's a bell to summon him if you need it. Clay will need fluids and we'll leave a pain pill. Otherwise, rest is what he needs most. He has been through an ordeal."

Rebecca bid good-bye and followed Dr. Burke into where Clay lay asleep.

It was dark outside when Lilly, Josiah and the girls left the Hawthorne House.

"Josiah, let's go to the train station and see if there is a late train. We can leave the horse and buggy at Mr. Hardesty's livery and come for them tomorrow. It's too late to ride to Boyce."

Lilly and the girls went inside the station where the girls sat on a bench while Lilly went to the station master.

"There's a 9:50 freight due. It doesn't stop in Boyce and doesn't take passengers."

Lilly was persistent. "Do you think they will make an exception?"

"Depends on the engineer," the man answered. "If not, you can sleep here in the station until morning."

She went out to where Josiah waited. "There's a freight train but it doesn't stop in Boyce. Maybe they will make an exception. If worse comes to worst, we can sleep overnight here. Drive the buggy to the stables. The girls and I will wait here."

The train arrived and the station master stopped the engineer when he came into the station for a short break. They talked quietly and looked over at four bedraggled persons sitting together on the bench. The station master came to where they sat. "Walt says you four can ride in the caboose with the help."

"How much will it cost?" asked a tentative Josiah.

"Walt says he has to pull the caboose anyway and your family looks like they've had a hard day. Won't cost a cent."

Josiah's family? Lilly didn't correct him.

Neither did Josiah. "Thank you, sir."

"Go ahead and get settled because they'll pull out in a couple of minutes. I'll tell Walt you're aboard."

Josiah hurried them along and the four climbed up into the caboose.

In Boyce they hurried off the train and waved to the engineer. He blew the train whistle once.

The day had been so filled with doubt and worry that even Emily didn't complain when they had to walk to *Roseville*.

Lilly rushed the girls off to bed and told them to say an extra prayer for Clay.

Josiah stood in the kitchen. "Are you all right, Lilly?"

"Now that I'm home."

"We are a strong pair together," he said. "I'll get my own breakfast, you need sleep."

"Good night, Josiah."

"Good night, Lilly."

Chapter 48

Rebecca stayed at the Hawthorne House with Clay for two solid days. On the third day, she walked to his big place east of town to freshen up before she walked back to the Hawthorne House. Clay said he was fine to be by himself, but she wouldn't hear of it. He also told her she shouldn't be walking that distance. She said it did her good to stretch her legs and let her mind wander as she walked.

After ten days the doctors said Clay was able to go home, but he was to take it easy and work up to crutches. They had left a hole in the plaster cast where they had stitched the area. It was clean with no sign of infection which made everyone happy. They cut off the cast he was wearing and replaced it with one that would cover the incision to make the cast more stable.

Lilly kept in touch by telephoning. When it was the day to be discharged, Josiah was to pickClay up at the Hawthorne House. Lilly and the girls would ride with him and visit at Laura's while Josiah brought Clay and Rebecca back.

Rebecca asked Lilly to bring clothes and personal items because she was going to stay with Clay until he was able to get around by himself.

Lilly thought that made sense. With Clay's leg in bad shape, it was unlikely there would be any reason for tales to be spread. Josiah said Clay and Rebecca had to work things out. Lilly was still concerned.

With Rebecca gone, Lilly was back to fixing all the meals, doing the laundry, ironing and tending the vegetable patch. Emily and Flossie were now ten and eleven, old enough to shoulder some of the load. Lilly didn't want to work them too hard. They were still children. She had seen other young girls old before their time.

Lilly thought about what Josiah had suggested about raising cattle and getting rid of the sheep. It sounded like a good plan. It would be less work for him and, God knows, he needed an easier path. Why she waffled about the change she didn't know. Josiah wouldn't have mentioned it if he didn't think it was best for her.

Next week it would be haying season again. Hay and tomatoes. They came at the hottest time of the year. Rebecca had put in twenty-five tomato plants and now she wouldn't be home to help with the canning. Lilly sighed at the thought. When things begin to brighten up another cloud appears. She never had to do the drudgery when Frank was alive. She hired people to do the heavy work. Now she couldn't even afford to hire a part-time man to help Josiah. What if Josiah broke his leg? Where would she be then? It was too much to think about.

**

Josiah drove Jack and the buggy to the back of the house. Lilly and the girls were excited about going. Lilly patted Ef and put her on the side porch. "We'll be back," she said. Then looked around to be sure no one heard her talking to a dog.

When they reached Laura's, Lilly's sister was waiting on the porch fanning herself with a magazine. The girls jumped out. Josiah came around to help Lilly down. He waved to Laura, hopped up to the seat and headed Jack back the way they came.

"It's too hot to be inside," said Laura, after Lilly greeted her with a hug. "Let's sit out under the trees."

Emily and Flossie found Sarah Jane and the three went out to play. "Don't go too far," cautioned Laura.

"We won't." Off they ran.

Lilly and her sister sat under the cooler trees. Lilly removed her hat and sat it on a tree stump that had been planed and lacquered to use as a seat.

"I've got cold sandwiches and potato salad for lunch," said Laura. "I should have offered you something to drink."

"I can wait for lunch. How are things going around here without Clayton?"

"You know John can run this place by himself."

Lilly smiled. "I figured that. Clayton's heart isn't in it."

"Where is Clay's heart? He seemed right fond of that Amish girl."

Laura referring to Rebecca as 'that Amish girl' lit a spark in Lilly. "Her name is Rebecca and she is no longer Amish. Besides what difference does that make?"

"None. I wanted to get a rise out of you."

"Darn it Laura, you still know how to needle me."

Laura laughed. "That isn't hard. I know Rebecca has been a big help to you and I think she is good for Clay."

"I miss her," lamented Lilly. "She's going to come and stay with Clayton until he can do for himself."

"He's going to need someone. Faith can cook and take care of the house but she isn't a nursemaid."

Lilly changed the subject. "Laura, Josiah said I should get rid of the sheep and start raising cattle. I've been struggling to make a decision since he mentioned it. Frank made a go of wool and sheep."

"And left you in debt. You sold off his wool business. I think your hired man makes a lot of sense."

"Don't call Josiah a hired man."

Laura raised an eyebrow. "Defending him as much as his sister?"

"I don't know where I'd be without him."

"Keep that in mind," advised Laura. "You never told me about your trip to New York City."

Lilly was all smiles. "It was pure luxury." Then she told Laura every detail.

Laura closed her eyes and leaned her head back on the chair. "It sounds like a dream." She sat up when Lilly finished. "What about this Tony? I met him when he was here. He seems a little too sly for me."

Lilly chuckled. "I think it's his city ways. He is kind and considerate. He sent me a note last week that he will be coming down to check on the foal he and his friend bought. They will be taking him to start training in a couple of months."

"Is that the foal Clay bought from you?"

"The same. I have three foals that Josiah suggested could be sold."

Laura scoffed, "Maybe this Tony and his friend from the big city will pay you a big price for them."

"Don't be cynical. Josiah said I could buy bred cows with the money. It will be a tight winter but a good start in the spring. What do you think?"

"I think you should take Josiah's advice, and be cautious around this Tony."

"Right now I can't think of anything except that the tomatoes and other crops in the garden will be ready for canning next week. The hayers are coming in ten days."

Laura nodded. "Who said we don't lead exciting lives. How about lunch?"

"I'm ready," answered Lilly.

Chapter 49

"I should go down and help Miss Lilly can the tomatoes," Rebecca said to Clay. "It is going to be too much work for her to do alone."

"Go ahead. Faith is here if I need anything."

"You are not steady on those crutches and I know you will try to be up."

"I'm tired of laying and sitting around."

"Why don't I drive you down in the wagon? You can play cards and checkers with Emily and Flossie. It will keep them busy and it will get you out of the house."

"I wish that Model T sitting out there worked and you could drive it."

"I don't drive cars and the men who brought it home said they didn't know if it could be fixed."

"I know." Clay was getting dejected about his limited mobility.

Rebecca came and knelt next to the chair where he sat. "I am good at driving a wagon and I can fix it up so you will be comfortable."

"I would be laying out with the hot sun beating down on me."

"I was thinking that I could stretch a piece of canvas across the back rail of the buckboard. I could sew an iron rod across the top and tie the sides to the wagon. That will give you shelter."

Clay cupped her chin in his large hand. "You have given this much thought." Then he kissed her.

A crimson glow came to Rebecca's face and she started to get up.

"Don't leave," he said, and placed his hand over hers. "I couldn't help but kiss you. Are you sorry?"

She relaxed. "No. But I have been taught that I am to keep myself from temptation until I am with the man I am to marry."

"What makes you think I am not that man?"

"Because we lead different lives. You still talk about going back to the university and owning your own drug store. If it is what you truly want, you should do it." She rose and sat in a chair next to him.

"I have an obligation to my father to keep this farm going."

"Why don't you let John Richards run it for you? Could you afford to go back to school without selling this place?"

"I'm not sure. I never gave that thought." Rebecca had planted a seed in his mind. "I guess Alex could help me sort that out. It would take at least two more years of schooling."

Rebecca leaned forward and took his hand. "Wouldn't the two years be worth it? You will do what you want to do and still own this place. I want you to be happy, Clay, and you aren't happy now."

"It's this bum leg."

"No, it isn't. This accident has made you slow down and look at your life. This is not what you want."

He squeezed her hand. "What has made you so wise?"

She slid her hand from his and sat back. "I was going to be forced to marry an old man I didn't even like. That opened my eyes."

Clay sat and thought. "If I go back to the university where will you be?"

"I will stay with Miss Lilly and do as I have done or there might be others who need my help."

"Find another old man who needs your help with a son who falls in love with you?"

Rebecca opened her eyes wide and her jaw dropped. "Do you know what you are saying?"

"I wouldn't say it if I didn't mean it. Could you wait for me to get my life in order?"

She flew from the chair and touched her forehead to his. "I could wait for you forever." This time she kissed him. "What do you say about my idea with the wagon?"

He laughed. "Let's go scare the living daylights out of your Lilly and Josiah!"

Chip Richards helped Rebecca fix up the wagon. She had to sew two more rods into the sides of the canvas to hold it up. She sewed the top rod far enough back that it allowed a flap to drop down for more shade. It took two days and her hands were sore.

The next morning, just after sun-up, she helped Clay out of the house. He was tall enough that he could sit on the back of the wagon. Rebecca's height and strength were a blessing. She stood at the side of the wagon and placed a hand under the injured leg while Clay wiggled his heavy torso to the front under the canvas.

Rebecca had placed pillows and piled blankets to keep him comfortable. "I have water in the jug beside you."

"You're sure you're good at driving this thing?"

She offered a wry smile. "I trust the wheel won't fall off like it did on your car."

"You don't have to remind me. Let's get on our way while it's still as cool as the day is going to get."

The wagon creaked and groaned all the way to Boyce. Lilly was looking out the kitchen window and let out a shout. "It's Rebecca!"

Emily and Flossie were out gathering tomatoes in the garden. They set down their pails and came running. "Rebecca," they both shouted.

She pulled the wagon to where it would be easier for Clay to get out. The girls looked in the wagon.

Lilly flew out of the kitchen door.

"Look, Momma," said Flossie. "Rebecca gave Mister Clay a ride."

Clay laughed. "Rebecca said we needed to come and help can tomatoes."

"Oh, Clayton. How are you doing? I hope this wasn't too much for you," said a concerned Lilly.

"I was going stir crazy," he answered.

"What's that mean?" asked Emily.

"I'll explain later," said her mother. "Can I help?"

"Rebecca and I have a routine."

"Clay is doing well with the crutches but he still needs steadying." Rebecca smiled up at Clay and Lilly could see admiration in her eyes.

Her worst fears were realized. Rebecca was in love with Clayton Lockwood.

They settled Clay under the tree and propped his bad leg up on a chair.

Emily and Flossie eagerly went back to picking tomatoes because Clay was going to play games with them when they were finished.

Lilly and Rebecca went into the hot kitchen, which was going to get even hotter to put up jars of tomatoes. Lilly also had onions and peppers from the garden. They would make jars of stewed tomatoes also.

Chop, chop, slice, slice, peel, peel, until it was time for lunch. They put slices of turkey, ham, cheese and tomatoes on a plate with a basket of sliced bread. If anyone wanted to make a sandwich they could make their own. They had boiled eggs, pickles and pepper slaw salad. Rebecca had brought ginger cookies.

Emily and Flossie cleaned off the outdoor table and put a tablecloth over it before they laid plates and utensils down.

Josiah came from the barn. He washed up at the well and sauntered over to where Clay sat.

He shook his hand. "I'm a bit surprised to see you two," he said.

"This is Rebecca's idea," informed Clay.

Josiah smiled. "I believe it is a good one. How are you doing?"

"I'm learning to navigate on the crutches. Another four weeks before the cast comes off."

"It needs to knit back together," said Josiah, and went to sit at the table.

They sat on benches around the table except for Clay. Rebecca filled his plate and took it to him.

"I've wormed the sheep again and I'm getting the barn ready for the hay next week."

"I can come and help Miss Lilly when you bring in the hay," offered Rebecca.

"That would take a load off my mind. Are you sure you can leave Clayton for a few days?"

"He is doing so well on his crutches, I don't think he will need my help after this week."

"Where did you get that idea?" called Clay.

"You are doing very well," said Rebecca. "Next week it will be time for me to move back to *Roseville*." She left no doubt that's the way it would be.

Emily and Flossie shouted, "Yea, we want you back."

After lunch Lilly and Rebecca went back to their work. The girls brought cards and Clay played Old Maid with them.

The he suggested,"Why don't you two come out to the barn with me? I want to see those other foals your mother has."

The two were all for it. Wherever Clay wanted to go they wanted to be with him.

Josiah was in the barn. He came to the horse stalls when Clay hobbled in on his crutches.

"Tony might be interested in another of Mrs. Pierce's foals. He will be down week after next to take a look at them. He seemed to think she is interested in selling them."

Josiah didn't say anything but he wondered.

Lilly and Rebecca worked until supper. Lilly had made a pot roast with vegetables and Rebecca made apple grunt. She and Clay stayed to eat before it was time to get the wagon back to Berryville while the sky was still light.

Lilly hugged Rebecca. "Thank you so much. The little that is left I can do in the morning. You must be exhausted."

"Once I get Clay home and settled, I will sleep very sound."

Clay looked comfortable propped with pillows and blankets in the back of the wagon.

"It appears Rebecca is taking good care of you, Clayton."

"I hope for a long time," was his reply.

After supper, Josiah told Lilly what Clay had said about Tony wanting to buy a foal.

She was honest. "Tony wrote and said he would be coming to check on the foal Clay is stabling for him. I wrote back and told him he might be interested in one of mine. I have decided that I should sell them and buy bred cows as you suggested."

A wide smile appeared. "You won't be sorry, Lilly."

"Can you buy some good stock for me?"

"I'll take Robert Graves with me. He works up on the Mitchell farm and he knows cattle."

"Graves? I know his wife. She used to help Miss Catherine in the hat shop. Mary......Mary Lee Thompson. She's a sweet person. Her first husband was killed by a train right at the crossing in Berryville. Everyone knew about that."

He smiled. "I didn't. I guess that's how people get to know other people's business."

"Did I sound like I was being a gossip?"

"No. Stating facts. When is Tony coming?"

"Wednesday. Not next week, the week after."

"How do you feel about him coming?"

"I wish I could answer that question."

Josiah put on his hat and turned to leave. "You may have answered it."

Chapter 50

Rebecca arrived on Tuesday and said she was home for good. Clay was able to get around on the crutches and it was time for her to return home.

On Wednesday the men came to help with the hay. Only two of their wives came. They were older women. One brought a pie and the other brought a three layer cake. Rebecca and Lilly had cooked pork roasts, mashed potatoes, baked beans, corn on the cob, green beans, pot pie and salads. There were eight men and they needed a big meal.

Once Lilly's hay was in, Josiah would make the circuit and help the farmers who had helped him. Rebecca, with Emily and Flossie's help, offered to take over Josiah's chores with the animals while he went to hay-it.

Lilly was busy making school clothes. Next week was the beginning of September and the girls would be back in school. Josiah said Robert was lined up to go to an auction and he would buy a couple of cows for her. She needed to sell the foals or she wouldn't have money for the October mortgage payment. Money was always a worry.

The next week Tony arrived on Wednesday as he said he would. Lilly was waiting. She wore a faint touch of rouge and face powder. Her hair was neatly rolled under with a flowered headband. She wore the French blue dress she had worn in New York. Rebecca had taken Emily and Flossie out in the fields to gather wild grapes for jelly.

Lilly's heart was aflutter when she heard the car come up the drive. It wasn't Clay's Model T.

She didn't wait for Tony to knock on the door, nor was she prepared for the car. As she stood open-mouthed, Tony got out dressed in a linen suit, wing-tipped shoes, spats and boater hat. Dashing.

"Do you like it? It's a brand new Mercedes-Benz touring car. I drove it down from New York." While she was still overcome, he wrapped her in his arms. "I have missed you."

Lilly felt like she might swoon. Tony was so likeable and unlikeable at the same time. She withdrew from his embrace.

"Lilly, the minute you left New York, I wanted to snatch you right back. It has taken all of my will-power to wait this long to come."

"I thought your reason for coming was to check on the foal at Clayton's. Have you been there?"

"The foal was a good excuse. Clay can wait. Can we go sit on that bench?"

He took her hand as they walked to the bench under the tree where they sat side by side. "What did you think of the city, Lilly? Are you ready to go back for a couple of days? You couldn't get a good feel for it in two rushed days."

How was she going to tell him without hurting his feelings? "I have to say that it was a wonderful time. I also know it is not where I care to live. The high life is too fast and superficial for me. I'm a country girl, Tony, not like the women I saw in New York."

He kissed her fingers. "I know you're not. I'm crazy about you, Lilly. You need to give me a chance. I can give you a good life; a new life that could open like a flower in full bloom."

She smiled at him and placed her hand over his. "You flatter me, Tony. If I were young, not a widow with two children, I would hop in that fancy car with you and travel right back to New York. But I'm thirty-one years old and I have responsibilities. You are a temptation that is hard to resist."

"Then don't resist, Lilly, please."

"Stop, Tony, or you're going to make me cry. You came to see the foals I have, we had better get on with that."

Reluctantly, he rose from the bench, but he put his arm around her waist as they walked to the barn. She liked the feel of his arm around her. It made her feel secure.

While they were looking at the foals, Rebecca and the girls returned, each with a basket of wild grapes.

Rebecca smiled when she recognized Tony. "Hello."

"Hi, Rebecca. Going out to stomp some wine?"

"Rebecca's going to show us how to make grape jelly," informed Flossie.

"Isn't it easier to buy it at the store?" asked Tony.

"They don't sell wild grape jelly at the store," said Emily.

"My mistake," he apologized.

Ef came in with the trio but she didn't come sniffing and wagging her tail to Tony like she always did with Josiah and Clay.

"We'll go on to the house and get started. It is nice to see you, Tony. Thank you for the grand time we had in New York."

"That was my pleasure, Rebecca. I'm trying to convince Lilly that she needs to come back again. There are still plenty of sights to see."

Flossie held an anxious look. "You're not going away, are you Momma?"

"No, Flossie, I'm not. I'll be along to the house in a few minutes."

When they left, Tony was downcast. "You're not coming back. I heard it in your voice."

"I know where I belong. This isn't an easy life, but it's my life. You'll find the right person for you. Are you interested in one of these foals or was that a pretense to come?"

"Lilly Pierce, you do come to the point. I did come to check on the foal Clay is holding and make arrangements for it to be shipped. My partner says we are steady and don't need another foal. You were right. It was an excuse to get to see you. I will go away disappointed, but I can see there is no need for me to return."

She walked with him to the sleek, black car just like ones she had seen in New York City driven by tough-looking men. "I wish you luck, Tony. Stay safe."

He got into the driver's seat and rolled down the window. "Are you sure you won't change your mind?"

"I won't change my mind."

"I leave with a broken heart."

Tony Vello was hard to resist, but she ignored his plea. "Believe me, your heart will heal." She watched as he drove away.

Josiah came in for supper that evening after a long, hot day. While they were eating, Rebecca told them that Clay was going back to the university.

"Alex told him to cash in some stocks that were in Clay's name. That way he can keep the farm and let John Richards run it."

"I'm glad," was Lilly's reaction. "It's what Clayton has wanted to do. Maybe that accident he had was God-sent to help him make up his mind."

"That isn't all he's made up his mind about," said a shy Rebecca. "He has asked me to wait for him, which I plan to do. Clay has already checked in with the university and he will go next week."

"What about his leg? He still has a couple of weeks in the cast," said Lilly.

"Dr. Burke told him he could have it removed by a doctor in Charlottesville."

Josiah smiled. "Looks like things are working out for both of you."

Chapter 51

The girls were back in school. Rebecca was baking bread. Lilly took some mending outdoors, where she sat on the bench under the oak tree. Josiah had found buyers for the foals and he and Robert Graves had bought four bred cows for her. What would she do without Josiah?

In the mindless work of darning socks, thoughts swirled in her head. Laura said Charlie and Ella were going to be married in two weeks. Lilly hoped it would be a nice day.

October would be one year that Frank had been gone. The cold, drizzly day was vivid in her mind. He had left her in debt and unprepared for running a farm, but she had managed.

It might be a slim winter until spring arrives with rebirth. There will be one more season of wool and lambs before she sells the sheep.

Lilly planned to put her money into cattle. Josiah said it would save *Roseville* and she trusted his judgement. After the war the cities were booming. People had more money. She saw it in the restaurants and businesses in New York.

Josiah came by. "Mending socks, I see."

She looked up into his clear blue eyes and strong face, tanned by the summer sun

"Come sit down," she invited and sat the mending aside.

He took a seat beside her. "It's a pretty day."

"It is," she agreed.

Josiah sat for a long moment. "Lilly, is Tony coming back?"

"No."

"I'm happy to hear that."

"Why?"

"Because I have had my eye on you since the first day I drove Andrew Caldwell over here."

Lilly turned her head with raised eyebrows to look at him. "Except for that one time you hinted that you cared, you never let on."

"Your husband will be gone one year next month and that will allow you to be free. No guilt, which you would have had if I had let my feelings show. I worried about Clay's friend, Tony. I thought he might sweep you off your feet. He can certainly give you a richer life than I can, but..."

Lilly put her hand up. "Stop right there, Josiah. Tony seems to have plenty of money and he lives life to the fullest. I won't say I wasn't tempted to go with him. With Tony, it would be a fling and he'd be off to something or someone else. That isn't the life I want. I need someone who works beside me to make this farm survive. Someone who loves *Roseville* as much as I do. Someone who will accept my girls as his own. Someone who loves me for myself."

He was silent before he spoke, "You're honest. That's a tall order but I believe I qualify. We would make a great pair."

Lilly sighed deeply, "This has been a year of trials. You don't know how many times I wanted to throw my arms around you and feel the strength of yours around me. I have watched your warm and loving ways. I have also felt guilty with those thoughts because of Frank."

He gave her that sly endearing smile. "Just watch." He waved his arm in an arc to encompass the expanse of the farm. "Once another winter is past, spring will arrive and this place will come to life. Next month will be a year since your husband died. Must I wait another month to tell you how I feel about you?"

"No. You can tell me right now."

In a flash, he was on his feet and pulled her to him. "Will you marry me?"

If she was surprised she didn't hesitate. "Oh, yes, Josiah!"

He kissed her lightly. His smile was teasing. "Do you think November would be too soon to be married? That room over the porch is mighty cold in the winter."

Lilly laughed and gave a playful tap on his shoulder. "I think November would be perfect. I have been so lonely I don't think I could put in another long winter by myself."

The lady of the house marrying the hired man?

"There will be talk, you know."

She placed her arms around his neck. "We are not young, innocent, starry-eyed dreamers. We both have had ups and downs in life and I expect there will be more to come. When they do, I want you right there with me."

He kissed her with a long, warm and gentle kiss. "I love you, Lilly Pierce."

The tingle his kiss sent through her body made her feel alive. "I have been waiting a long time for you, Josiah Bly."

About the Author

Millie Curtis is a native of Oneida, New York and has made her home in the Shenandoah Valley of Virginia since 1975. She lives with her husband, one dog and one cat on two acres in the bucolic countryside of Clarke County. As with her other books, Roseville's Blooming Lilly is a bit of history, a bit of humor and a bit of romance.

CPSIA information can be obtained
at www.ICGtesting.com
Printed in the USA
FFHW02n0520270918
48568407-52485FF